SAMSON IN GAZA

TEX FORD

WESTBOW°
PRESS
A DIVISION OF THOMAS NELSON
& ZONDERVAN

Cover Art
"Samson in Gaza"
Chris Zeiher, 2012

Interior Art
Chris Zeiher, 2013

WestBow Press books may be ordered through booksellers or by contacting:

WestBow Press
A Division of Thomas Nelson & Zondervan
1663 Liberty Drive
Bloomington, IN 47403
www.westbowpress.com
1 (866) 928-1240

ISBN: 978-1-4908-2750-6 (sc)
ISBN: 978-1-4908-2751-3 (hc)
ISBN: 978-1-4908-2752-0 (e)

Library of Congress Control Number: 2014903466

Printed in the United States of America.

WestBow Press rev. date: 4/04/2014

To my mother, Marguerite, who birthed me.
To my father, Harold, who adored me.
To my sisters, Marguerite Dawn and Linda
Christine who sharpened me.
To my brother Jaime Ferris who befriended me.
To my teacher, Dorothy Jasiecki, who showed me.
To my wife, Linda Ford, who completed me.
To my children, Mandolin, Harold, Danielle,
and Chris, who endured me.
To my Lord God, Jesus Christ, who also did
all of the above and then saved me.

THUS SAITH THE LORD, LET NOT THE WISE MAN GLORY IN HIS WISDOM, NEITHER LET THE MIGHTY MAN GLORY IN HIS MIGHT, LET NOT THE RICH MAN GLORY IN HIS RICHES: BUT LET HIM THAT GLORIETH GLORY IN THIS, THAT HE UNDERSTANDETH AND KNOWETH ME, THAT I AM THE LORD WHICH EXERCISE LOVINGKINDNESS, JUDGEMENT, AND RIGHTEOUSNESS IN THE EARTH: FOR IN THESE THINGS I DELIGHT, SAITH THE LORD."
—JEREMIAH 9:23-24
FROM THE KING JAMES TRANSLATION OF THE BIBLE

CONTENTS

PROLOGUE..XI

MANOAH: THE FATHER 1

ZELPONI: THE MOTHER...6

ANGEL: THE LORD GOD... 11

SAMSON: THE BIRTH 19

SAMSON: THE BOY 23

SAMSON: THE MAN 33

MERARI: THE WIFE 42

PHICOL: THE COMMANDER 54

DELILAH: THE GODDESS 68

ZETHAM: THE PRIEST 89

PHICOL: THE GENERAL... 108

SAMSON: THE MAN OF GOD 115

SAMSON: THE TOMB 134

EPILOGUE...137

PROLOGUE

Samson stretched his arms and flexed his mighty muscles. He was standing on a hill overlooking the land of the Philistines. His body glistened in the sun from the oil he had rubbed on himself.

Samson reveled in his strength and the power it gave him over other men. He loved looking at the image that gazed back at him from the polished gold shield that hung on the wall in his father's house. His father had made it for him when he achieved manhood, and it was one of his most precious possessions because in it he could see himself. It was a long shield like the Philistines used, designed to protect a soldier from head to toe. Even now as a grown man, when Samson stood back a little distance from it, he could see his whole body reflected. He never tired of seeing himself and admiring his lean face; long braids of hair; and chiseled, smooth, and perfectly formed body.

Ever since he was a young boy, Samson had been acutely aware of his unusual strength. There were times when it was greater than what seemed humanly possible. At such times, he felt as though he could lift the world on his shoulders. His father and mother had told him this was because his strength had come from God, and that God expected him to use that strength only for good. However, Samson was not sure about this. He thought his strength was just a natural result of his being such a fine specimen of manhood. His strength did not extend into the trait of humility.

Samson didn't worry about trying to explain those unusual times of strength. In fact, he was not given to spending a lot of his energy in thinking. He was a man of action. Anyway, such things had never been important to him. Perhaps it was just a burst of power caused by his reaction to some provocation or to his surroundings. He didn't care. He just knew the strength was there when he needed it and called on it seemingly at the whim of his own mind.

From the time he was born, Samson had been told that the land he now surveyed was the land of his enemies. He was supposed to hate the Philistines with a passion, as they were the sworn enemy of his people, and he should want to humiliate if not destroy them. The priests who tried to train him taught him that he should look for every opportunity to cause the Philistines trouble and expected it would be one of the great pleasures of his life.

In truth, Samson did not hate the Philistines at all. What feeling he did have for them had nothing to do with their being the enemy of Israel. It was more the result of his pride. Since he had been told these people were his enemies, his pride urged him to shame them, make an example of them, and destroy them if possible. Is that not what strong men did to their enemies? Samson's parents had never spoken of the Philistines as their enemy. His father had prospered because of the Philistines, and his mother had no love for the priests, so it was no wonder that Samson did not hate the Philistines.

Samson had been chosen to be one of the judges of the Hebrew people, a position he did not relish. He had no desire to perform the task. After all, who was he to judge other people? The judges of Israel were traditionally military leaders called upon during conflicts with the other inhabitants of the land of Canaan to lead the people in battle. Samson had no taste for this. He was a loner. Yes, he loved to fight and enjoyed immensely besting an enemy, but he liked to do it on his own and not with other people helping him. This allowed him greater pride in the victory that inevitably came.

Now he made regular forays into the land of the Philistines. He was not looking for ways to torment them. He just craved a challenge and hungered for the thrill of new things. His father, Manoah, had cautioned him about this and told him that always wanting something new would lead him into trouble. Manoah was a hardworking and industrious man. He had labored at building up his business so he could give Samson all that his heart desired. Perhaps that was a weakness in Manoah. But Samson didn't think so.

Samson yawned, and smiling, he looked down over the land spread out beneath him. From this vantage point, he could see a vast expanse of Philistine territory and felt he was the master of it all. Wanting another adventure, Samson began to make his way along the narrow path that meandered out of the hills.

MANOAH: THE FATHER

Manoah struck the base of the sword repeatedly with his hammer, drawing it slowly out to its proper length.

"Manoah, you son of a Danite dog. Quit wasting time with that sword, and get over here!"

Manoah worked for a harsh man, Perez, who loved to remind Manoah of his lowly position as an apprentice. Perez came from what was called the royal line of the tribe of Judah. He never missed an opportunity to point that out to Manoah.

The one thing Manoah liked about Perez was that he had a beautiful daughter named Zelponi. She was nothing like Perez, so Manoah thought she must be like her mother. Perez told him Zelponi's mother had died when Zelponi was just a young girl. Perhaps this had helped Manoah to fall in love with her the first moment he saw her. She had been standing in the doorway of her father's house when Manoah had first come to stay with them and begin his apprenticeship. He thought she looked like such a lonely and sad little creature. His heart went out to her, and as he got to know her father, his sympathy and love for her grew.

Zelponi had assumed a slight air of haughtiness and indifference toward other people. This may have been her defense against the ache and emptiness in her heart that began when her mother died. She still had a vague impression in her mind of her mother's face—warm, soft, and loving, with a glow of hazy light around it. It was a face that was always smiling, and when Zelponi imagined it, she felt warm and secure inside.

Manoah's father, Ammiel, had instructed Manoah that being a blacksmith was a noble profession. "You will never go hungry in such a job," his father had said. "Blacksmiths are always in demand. People constantly need new farming tools, and they need the old ones sharpened and repaired. They need their horses shod and their weapons forged."

Ammiel was a proud man. He had worked his little plot of land just outside the small village of Zorah for years, toiling at the soil to produce food for his family. He sold his grains and vegetables at the market in Zorah to make his living, sometimes barely making enough to pay for the seed he had to buy each year. In the years of drought, he was happy to grow enough to put food on his table. He wanted more for Manoah, his only child. He wanted him to be free of the land that was so often unproductive. Manoah recalled hearing his father muttering to himself as he worked on his farm, which often sounded like he was questioning the description of their land as the land of milk and honey.

The answers to Ammiel's questions were readily available from the priest of Zorah, who said that the land was under a curse because of the unfaithfulness of the Israelites. Some in Zorah had begun to worship the sun god, praying to it so it might smile on them and give them prosperity in the harvest and in their trade. The priest warned Ammiel not to fall into the trap of worshipping false gods, but Ammiel did not understand it all. Some said the village was named after the sun god. But Ammiel was not concerned with such things. He just wanted to take care of his family.

"The people are doing what is right in their own eyes," the priest told Ammiel. "They have forgotten the law of God. Did the Lord God not tell Moses that He would send curses to us if we failed to obey the law? Now the curses have come."

Making weapons was what Manoah loved. He delighted in producing beautiful swords and spears that glinted and shone in the sun. He cared nothing for working on farm implements. However, in times of peace, that was where the money was to be made, so Perez was constantly calling him back to the main work of the shop and away from his side projects of making swords.

Manoah walked over to Perez, who was forging the frame of a new oxcart. "Yes, Master? How can I help you?"

"Stand over there, and help me lift this cart onto the frame."

Manoah walked around the cart and helped Perez lift it to its position on the frame where the wheels were mounted.

"There, that's better," said Perez. "Why do I have to keep calling you to help me, Manoah? You don't seem to understand that an apprentice is a helper. It is your job to be here when I need you and to do as you are told. Yet I constantly find you fooling around, making poor quality swords and knives."

"Oh, but they are not poor quality, Master. I am perfecting my technique every day."

"You are a fool, Manoah." Perez spat on the ground. "Just who do you think will buy those swords when you are done?"

"There is always a demand if the quality is good, Master."

"Oh? Where is this demand? I have not heard of it. Do you think I would waste time on oxcarts and plows if swords were selling? Listen to me, Manoah. When the people of Israel came into this great land of ours, we came with swords and spears. We needed them while crossing through the desert to help us defeat our enemies along the way. But those times are behind us. Now we need plows, winnowing forks, winepresses, saws, and nails. That is what will build up this land, not weapons! Maybe you want to sell them to our enemy the Philistines?"

"That is exactly who would buy them, Master! They love weapons, and they will pay dearly for them."

"Oh? Well, that certainly makes it a good idea. Let's just sell more weapons to our enemies so they can kill us easier, eh? Anyway, just how do you know they would buy them, my little apprentice? Who has been talking to you and putting such crazy notions in your head? I know you have not been so foolish as to go down through the valley to find out such information." The valley of Sorek ran below the village and stretched south into the land of the Philistines.

Manoah had never dared to go to the valley and was hesitant to answer. In truth, he had no idea if the Philistines would buy his weapons, although he had heard they would from his young friend

Micah. Micah was a dreamer. He loved to talk of going to war with the Philistines and defeating them in a great battle. He had gone with his father, who was a merchant that sold goods to the Philistines. He traveled with large caravans of other merchants down into the valley and to the cities of their sworn enemies. Micah was proud of his father, who only saw the Philistines as trading partners and had no fear of them.

In reality, the relationship between the Philistines and the Israelites was generally peaceful. The people of Israel had mingled with the Philistines, and they found each other to be good customers. The Israelites were often blessed with abundant crops. They were also expert weavers, and the clothes they made were like gold in the land of Canaan. The Philistines hungered for merchandise from Israel, so they put on the appearance of wanting peace so they would not endanger their trade.

But this trade enraged the priests. They tried instilling fear of the Philistines into the people so they would stop trading and living in such harmony with them. The priests knew that the ungodliness of the Philistines was infectious, resulting in the Israelites turning away from their God. However, the Philistines had fine cities and gold and silver. They were a snare to the Israelites who wanted their goods if not their gods.

Micah came back from his travels with different tales of the Philistines than those told by the priests. He told of their riches and their love for weapons. They had many fine blacksmiths among them, and they scorned the people of Israel for not making weapons for themselves. His stories had fired Manoah with zeal to produce even more than he had in the past. His little store of swords had reached what seemed to him an enormous number: five in all. These swords were precious to him, especially since Perez took some of his pay each month to cover the cost of the metal he used to create them. But Manoah didn't mind. Micah had promised that when Manoah had enough swords, he and his father would take them along on their next trip to see if they could be sold. Manoah did not wish for Perez to know of this arrangement, as he would look like quite a fool if the Philistines refused to buy his work.

"Nobody has put them in my head," Manoah finally responded. He looked down at his feet as he spoke, hesitant to meet Perez's eyes for fear that Perez would see the lie in his. "I just believe that if we produce good things, surely someone out there will want to buy them. They will buy the weapons just so they can strap them to their sides and show them off to each other. You know how the Philistines love to boast about their power. My swords will just give them something more to boast about!"

Perez sighed and continued working on the oxcart. "Alright, Manoah. I won't stop you from wasting your pay, but you do it on your own time, not during our working hours. Do you understand?"

"Yes, Master! Yes, yes!"

Manoah was elated. Perez's grudging agreement was the first encouragement he had ever given him in the four years Manoah had served of his ten-year apprenticeship. Maybe there was hope for him to marry Zelponi after all. If he could sell the swords for a good price, Perez would have to admit that Manoah was a smart businessman as well as an able blacksmith. Then perhaps he would not be so critical of Manoah and be willing to hear of an engagement between him and Zelponi.

Zelponi, in the meantime, had no idea of the possibility of such an engagement. Manoah had hardly spoken to her since coming to live in her father's house, or rather in his shop, for that is where Manoah slept, in a little room in the back. The forge was in a low building just a few yards from the side of their house. Manoah had been too shy and unsure of himself to say a word to Zelponi. She would have been quite surprised to know the thoughts that were going through his head at that moment.

Manoah was certain that Perez wished to find a fine rich man to marry his daughter. After all, a good bride price could pay the foundry's expenses for some time and leave a nice profit in Perez's purse. Manoah had previously thought that there was little hope of Zelponi becoming his wife. He didn't think he could ever raise enough to please Perez. Now, however, his hope was kindled, and he felt a pounding in his chest at the thought of having such a beautiful woman as his wife. Manoah resolved to work even harder at producing the weapons.

ZELPONI: THE MOTHER

Zelponi sat in the kitchen of her father's house, kneading some barley flour into a ball. She added a few drops of olive oil and wine to the mixture. This gave the bread a smooth and yet tart flavor that her father enjoyed. After the bread was in the stone oven, she started to grind some dates into a paste and blend it together with goat's milk for the evening's porridge. Her mind was not on the preparation of the meal, however. It was on Manoah.

Early in the morning of the previous day, he had come into the kitchen and spoken to her. He had never entered the kitchen before, other than at mealtime when he joined her and her father at the table. Even then, he would only come when she tapped on the bottom of one of her cooking pots to let the men in the forge know the meal was ready. Manoah stood in the doorway to the kitchen at the back of the house, looking at her, as she put little dabs of honey on the bread for the morning meal.

"What is it, Manoah?"

"I have come to speak with you."

"Well, I am here, so speak."

"I am not sure what to say."

"You said you came to speak with me. How can you come to speak with nothing to say?"

"I did not say that I had nothing to say. I am just not sure how to say it."

"Just speak, Manoah. If you have something to say, just say it."

"I want you to be my wife."

Zelponi laughed, and her dark eyes flashed brightly. Her infectious laugh made Manoah smile, even though it was not encouraging to his proposal.

"You want me to be your bride? What has brought this on?"

"I am not sure."

Zelponi made a sound like a short cough in her throat. "Then you hardly want to marry me! What woman wants a man who is not sure?"

"You keep twisting my words, Zelponi. I am sure of *why* I want to marry you. I love you! I just am not sure what brought it on. That is what you asked me, isn't it? But I am not sure at this moment."

"Well, then perhaps it is not the time to speak of it."

"It is, Zelponi, it is! Perhaps I do know why I am speaking now! I am not getting any younger. I am already twenty-six years old! Your father told me that you were fifteen when I came here. Since I have been here for six years now, you must be twenty-one years old and you have grown to be a beautiful woman. Some man from the village will come any day soon and ask your father for you as his bride, and then it will be too late for me."

Zelponi made a blowing sound with her lips. "You make it sound as though I will jump at the first man who comes through the door! If I am as beautiful as you say, I can afford to wait and choose whom I please, can I not?"

"Yes, Zelponi. Yes, of course, you can. I ... I did not mean to say ... that is ... I ... Well, I am sorry that I am so clumsy. I could not wait. I have loved you since the first day I set foot in the forge. I remember you brought some water out for your father to drink. Even in the darkness of the forge, I saw a light on your face as if from heaven. The light of an angel in the smoky shop of a blacksmith."

Zelponi looked at Manoah intently, and then she smiled. "So you **can** put two words together. My father said you couldn't."

"Is that what he told you?"

"Yes, but you mustn't tell him I told you. He would not be pleased with me for saying it. He said you couldn't put two words in a row that made any sense. He said your speech was halting like father Moses, and that you needed an Aaron to speak for you."

This seeming betrayal of her father's criticism about him gave Manoah some hope. Would she open her heart to him in this manner, almost speaking against her father, if she did not care for Manoah? He felt heat around his forehead, and his chest burned.

"I am sorry he feels that way," Manoah said, looking away from her. "I am not a bold person, Zelponi. At least not most of the time. I can speak when I have to, but sometimes the words do not come out right."

"Well, don't worry yourself about it. Today they came out just fine, Manoah. Still, I do not know if I will marry you or not. First you must tell me what you have to offer me besides love. Love is fine. All women want to be loved. But we also want to be taken care of. How will you do that? I do not want to spend the rest of my life as the wife of a blacksmith. I am sorry, and I mean no disrespect to you or my father, but that is how I feel. I do not think I am greedy, but I want to be able to hold my head up high in the marketplace. I want to give good things to my children and make them proud of me. That is the role of every good parent, is it not?"

"I suppose so."

"Well, you should suppose so. Your father was a farmer, another noble profession, mind you, but he wanted you to learn a trade and escape from the life of the farm."

"Who told you that my father was a farmer?"

"My father did, of course. He does tell me some things, though not many."

"There is nothing wrong with working on a farm," Manoah said sullenly. "If nobody did, where would we get our food?"

"That is not my point," Zelponi said, her voice rising. She shook her head and tossed back her long, black hair. "I was just trying to say that every parent should want more for their children than they had. Is that not what the law teaches?"

"I am not a priest, Zelponi. You would have to ask one of them about the law."

"You know what I mean, Manoah."

"Yes, Zelponi. I know what you mean, and I want to give good things to our children also."

"Ha! You speak as though we were already married," Zelponi said with a laugh.

"I wish we were," Manoah sighed. "But I know you can choose who you like. I only ask you to choose me. As to what I can give you, soon I will be able to give you a great deal. Perhaps your father does not speak of the forge business with you. I thought he would have since your mother died and he has nobody else to speak to in the evenings. The forge has been doing very well since I started selling weapons to the Philistines. In the last two years, I have made twenty trips to their cities with Micah and his father. We have sold swords and spears and have taken orders for armor in all of those cities. The forge is prospering as a result, and your father shares the profits with me. At first, all of the profits were mine, as I made the weapons from my own wages. Then when your father saw the volume of business, he asked me to include him, and we became partners. I paid him a king's ransom for the four years of apprenticeship that I still owed him."

Zelponi raised her eyebrows at this. Then she looked away from Manoah and took in a long, deep breath. "No, he does not discuss those things with me," she said. "I wish he would."

"Do you ask him about them?"

"No, I don't. Since my mother died, he has not spoken to me very much. I suppose a part of him died with her. Anyway, he does not like to talk about his work, at least not to me, so I do not ask."

"When you marry me, I will talk to you about my work, and soon it will not be the work of the forge. I will retire from there, and we can do as we please."

"You are very bold all of a sudden. Who said I would marry you?"

"I think you will. I may not be the greatest suitor in the land of Israel, but I love you. I will take care of you, treat you well, and speak to you every night. Just wait and see."

"Yes, I shall wait and see. Now you better get back to work, Mr. Wealthy Blacksmith."

Manoah left the kitchen, smiling.

That night, Zelponi slept fitfully. She awakened several times, shivering with fear. She did not like the darkness of the nighttime.

Each time she awoke, Manoah's words ran through her head. She was getting older. Most girls her age had long before been betrothed and then married. She was suddenly afraid that nobody else would ever ask her. In any case, she thought having Manoah as a husband would not be a bad thing. He was a good-looking man, tall and muscular, and he did not smell bad. His teeth were good, and his arms must certainly be strong from the years in the forge. She wondered how his arms would feel around her. What would it be like to kiss him? He did not seem to have breath that would be putrid. Maybe she should accept him.

Now, a day later, pondering these thoughts as she prepared the meal for the night, Zelponi looked out the back door of the house and breathed deeply. She continued working on the bread mixture for the evening meal. The dough would be very well mixed.

ANGEL: THE LORD GOD

Zelponi lay in bed on her side. She looked out at the room with sightless eyes, staring as if she were looking into some great void, seeing nothing.

Manoah stood beside the bed, speaking to her in hushed tones. "You must get up, my love. I have made a nice breakfast for you."

"I am not hungry."

"Come, my darling. I plead with you to eat something."

"For what, Manoah? It is better that I starve and die. I am a barren woman. We have been married these three years and have no children. I was sad when my father died, thinking that he had not lived to see his grandchildren. Now I think perhaps it is best that he did not live to see his daughter's shame."

Perez had died within three months of Manoah's proposal. He had suffered with a cough for several weeks. Zelponi and Manoah begged him to go to the physician, but he refused. "I am a blacksmith," he had said. "We are expected to have coughs after years in the forge. It will go away. You act like two nursemaids. Go, and let me rest."

They had left Perez in his room, but Zelponi went back in an hour to check on him. She could not awaken him, and his breath came in short gasps. Manoah had sent for the priest and the physician from Zorah right away. Perez died within an hour of their arrival. Zelponi stayed by his side, sobbing and holding his hand until he drew his last breath.

"I do not wish to leave the house," Zelponi continued. "You know that the women in the marketplace mock me and laugh beneath their veils."

"Nobody would dare laugh if I was there."

"No, perhaps not. But you are not always there, are you? You cannot always be there, and when I am alone, I feel my shame worse than ever."

"But there is no shame, my love. Did not the priests say that many noble women of Israel have been barren first and then fruitful? What about father Abraham's wife?"

"You are quite mad if you think I want to have a child when I am ninety years old, like she did."

"I was just trying to make a point. God alone knows if He might deliver us from this barrenness. How do we know? Perhaps I am the one who is barren!"

"Hah! What man of Israel would admit such a thing? You never speak of men being barren, only of women!"

"I would speak of it," Manoah said softly. "I have spoken of it because I love you, Zelponi. If you are shamed, I am shamed. It matters not which of us is barren."

Zelponi looked at Manoah now, her eyes tender and filling with tears. "You are a good man, Manoah. No other man would say such a thing. I know you love me, but you cannot understand my shame. The other women shun me as though I had the plague. The priests and judges shun you, even though you are one of the wealthiest men in the tribe of Dan now. They came here and prayed over me. They made signs and burned smelly powder and spoke words I did not understand. For what, I ask you? For nothing, Manoah. It did nothing. Then they took you outside to tell you about my shame. They pretended they were going out with you to make a sacrifice on our altar, but they were fools. Did they think I could not hear their loud whispers? I heard every word, Manoah. 'She is barren, Manoah. We are sorry, Manoah. It is a curse from God, Manoah. She must have sinned, Manoah. Thank you for the offering, Manoah.' Yes, Manoah, I heard it all. And now we cannot escape the shame."

"I am sorry that you heard it, my love. I should have chased them all down the road to the city for their words. But I could not. My father taught me to respect and honor the priests. I do not understand them, but they are the keepers of the law. Now you must get up, my love. You cannot just stay in bed all the time. It will make you sick."

"I will be fine, Manoah. I am just tired now. I just want to sleep."

"Alright, you sleep then. I will go out to the fields for a while."

"Why do you insist on working in the fields, Manoah? I have never understood why you wanted to buy all that land and start farming like your father did. I thought you wanted to escape all of that. Now you are a prosperous man and have enough field workers to do everything. Why must you go out there?"

"I suppose it is my father in me, Zelponi. I grew up on my father's farm. I don't imagine those things you grow up with ever leave you. I only became a blacksmith to please my father. I had no desire for it. Now I am happy I became one, as it has made my fortune. Yes, Zelponi, we have plenty of workers to run the forge and the farmlands, but I love to walk in the fields. I love to be among the crops and see the fruit God has given us."

"Yes, I love to walk there also, but you go out there to work."

"Work keeps my mind busy and stops me from worrying about you."

"Yes, my love, yes. Go ahead then."

Shortly after Manoah left the house, Zelponi got up from the bed and went to sit by the rear door. They did not live next to the blacksmith shop any longer.

Manoah's work had made the shop famous for turning out fine armor and weapons. With the constant demand for more weapons from the Philistines, he had been able to employ many blacksmiths. He also hired a manger to oversee them. Customers now came from the far reaches of Israel. The men of Dan and Judah had begun to arm themselves as the Philistines were constantly at their borders, setting up settlements and pushing the boundaries of their territory.

Manoah had built their new house close to the forge. It was a large dwelling, standing on a low mound of earth overlooking the plains and hills beyond. In the evening, as the sun was going down in the western sky, Manoah and Zelponi would sit on the porch outside their back door. From there they would watch the last red streaks on the horizon turn to gold and then to gray. Zelponi sat there now. She put her head against the back of her chair and soon fell asleep. She slept for quite some time.

When Zelponi opened her eyes, she saw a man walking toward her along the path that led from the back of their house to the distant hills. He was dressed all in white with a crimson sash around his waist.

"Hail, Zelponi, wife of Manoah of Dan," the man said as he approached the house.

"Who are you?" Zelponi asked.

"I have come with a message for you."

"A message? Who sent me a message? Does my husband need me?"

"Your husband is working in the fields. This is a message from the Lord."

"From the Lord?"

"Yes. You will conceive and give birth to a son. The boy is to be raised as a Nazirite."

"Have the women of the town sent you to mock me?" Zelponi asked, anger in her voice. "I am barren and can have no children."

"Yes, you are sterile and childless, but you are going to conceive and have a son. You must prepare yourself. You are to drink no wine or other drink with fermentation, and you are to eat no unclean food. When your son is born, no razor is to touch his head, as he will be a Nazirite. He will be set apart for God from the time he is born. God will begin the deliverance of Israel from the hands of the Philistines through him." With that, the man turned to walk away, treading slowly back down the path.

"Wait!" cried Zelponi. "What should I tell my husband?"

But as suddenly as he had appeared, he was gone.

Zelponi blinked and strained to see in the distance, but he had disappeared. Now she wondered if she had been dreaming. She got up and put on her cloak and ran from the house. The grain fields were only a short distance from the house on the road to the village. She hurried to the fields and saw her husband there, talking to the workers. He had his back to her, but one of the men touched his arm and pointed to his wife coming down the road. Manoah ran to meet her.

"What is it, Zelponi?" he gasped. "Is anything wrong?"

She was out of breath from running. She grabbed onto Manoah's robe and clung to him. "A man came to the house," she blurted. "It was a man of God. He looked bright and awesome, like an angel. He was dressed in pure white clothes and had a sash of royalty around his waist. He came down the road behind our house. I was afraid. I didn't even ask him where he came from. He said to me that I would have a son, and that I was to drink no wine and eat nothing unclean. He said that the child would be a Nazirite of God from the time he is born until the day of his death."

"A Nazirite? That is like being a priest," Manoah said. "What was this man's name?"

"He did not say his name."

"Why didn't you ask him his name or where he came from?" Manoah asked, exasperated.

"I do not know. I told you I was afraid. Manoah, he glowed like the sun! He said that the boy should have no razor put on his head, and that God would begin the deliverance of Israel from the Philistines through him. I am afraid, Manoah. I do not understand what this means."

"Well, do not be afraid. We will pray and ask God what to do. Come, let us go back to the house so you can rest."

"Yes, I am tired again. I thought maybe it was a dream and no man came at all. But it was so real that I cannot believe it was a dream."

Manoah put his arm around Zelponi's shoulders, and they walked back to the house together. Zelponi lay down in their bed again and was soon asleep.

Manoah sat down at the table in the kitchen, put his head in his hands, and began to cry. His heart was hurting over this new thing. Who was this man? He resented that some man had come to his house while he was away. Had none of the servants seen him? He had not asked. He was afraid also. What if this was a man from God? What was he to do?

Finally, he stopped crying and whispered a prayer. "Oh Lord, I beg you, let the man of God you sent to us come again to teach us how to bring up the boy who is to be born." Manoah did not know why he prayed those words. They simply came into his head, and then he spoke them. He wasn't even sure that this was a man of God or that God had sent him.

Manoah slept fitfully that night and rose early in the morning to sit, as Zelponi had sat, at the back door. He hoped that the man would come again in response to his prayer. When Zelponi arose, they had a breakfast of sweet bread and dates.

"I will stay here today," said Manoah. "Perhaps this man from God will come again. I have prayed and asked the Lord God to send him."

"Yes, my husband. We will sit together and wait."

However, the man did not appear again. For two more days, Manoah and Zelponi sat faithfully on the back porch waiting for him, but he did not come. On the third day, Zelponi was cleaning up the bowls from their breakfast. She called out to Manoah, who was already sitting on the porch. "Maybe I should go out to walk in the fields. While I am gone, the man may come and talk to you."

"Yes, Zelponi, what you say is good," replied Manoah. "I will stay here."

Zelponi left the house and walked in the cool morning air down the road to the grain fields and the olive groves beyond. It was the Sabbath, and no workers were in the fields. After thinking about it for two days, she felt better about the message from the man of God. She was no longer afraid. What if she did have a son? What a wonderful thing it would be! As she walked, she looked out over the fields and saw a man among the stalks of grain.

"Hello!" she called out. "What are you doing there? It is the Sabbath. You are not to be in the fields today."

When the man walked out from among the stalks, she saw it was the same man from God. This time his entire garment was red. The cloth shone like the rare sheets of material she had seen in the marketplaces of Ekron.

"Hail, woman. I have come in response to your husband's prayer."

"You must speak to him. Will you come to the house with me?"

"No, I will remain here. You go and tell him I am here."

Zelponi turned and ran to the house. Manoah was still sitting on the porch, staring out to the pathway, watching for the man.

"Manoah!" she cried. "Come quickly! He's here! The man who appeared to me the other day. He is waiting in the fields for you."

Manoah jumped up from his chair and followed Zelponi to the fields. The man still stood there by the side of the road, watching them approach. "Hail, man of Dan," he called.

"Are you the one who talked to my wife?" Manoah asked, his voice trembling.

"I am," the man answered.

"You told her that she will have a child."

"Yes, and she will."

"When your words are fulfilled, what is to be the rule for the boy's life and work? How will we train him? We do not know what to do about the vow you spoke of."

"Have the priests not instructed you in the ways of God?"

"We do not talk to the priests very much. They shun people who are barren."

"Your wife must do all I have told her. She must not eat anything that comes from the grapevine, nor drink any wine or other fermented drink, and she must eat nothing that is unclean. She must do everything I have commanded her."

"Come to our house," Manoah begged. "We would like for you to stay with us until we can prepare a young goat for you."

"Even though you detain me," the man responded, "I will not eat any of your food. If you prepare a burnt offering, offer it to the Lord."

"What is your name? We wish to honor you when your words come true."

"Why do you ask my name? It is beyond your understanding."

Manoah bowed before the man. He felt a strange sense of fear and dread in this man's presence. He took Zelponi's hand and turned to walk back to the house. The man made no motion to follow them, so Manoah turned back toward him. "Come with us, please," Manoah entreated. "Come to our house."

Then the man followed, walking at a slower pace behind them. When they reached the house, he made no move to enter it but walked to the rear of the house and stood before the porch near the altar stone.

Behind their house was a low, flat rock. It was here that the priests had made an offering to God for Manoah and Zelponi that her barren womb would be opened. They had burned incense and grain on the rock and chanted and prayed. Yet nothing had happened.

Manoah sent one of the servant boys to get a young goat from the pen on the side of the house. He slaughtered it and carried it inside so Zelponi could prepare it to be roasted. When the goat was prepared, Manoah piled straw and sticks on top of the stone, set the goat on top of the pile, and placed some raisin cakes and grain around it. Then with a torch he set fire to the straw. Manoah looked up to heaven and prayed as Zelponi and the man from God watched. "Lord God in heaven, accept this sacrifice from your servant's hands, and show us the way to raise this child that you have sent your messenger to announce to us."

Then, without a word of warning, the man from God stepped forward and walked right up to the rock. He stepped up onto it and his body burst into a giant blaze of fire that shot up into the sky. Then the flame was gone. The goat was also gone. Not a trace of it or the other offerings was left on the rock. It was bare.

Manoah and Zelponi had stepped back when the fire blazed, but now they both fell with their faces to the ground. They stayed like that for some time, trembling in fear and half expecting to be consumed themselves. Finally, Manoah lifted his head slightly. "We are doomed to die," he whispered to his wife. "We have seen God Himself."

Zelponi looked up now also and, seeing nothing, got back up on her feet. Manoah stood up beside her.

"No, my husband. I do not think we will die. If the Lord had meant to kill us, He would not have accepted the offering from our hands. He would not have shown us these things and told them to us. Come, let us go into the house. We have to prepare a nursery room for our son."

SAMSON: THE BIRTH

The baby gave a loud cry as the midwife cleaned off the afterbirth and blood. He was a big strong boy with powerful lungs. Manoah beamed and watched with pride as Zelponi, soaked with sweat and exhausted from the birth, took her son, swaddled in the finest soft cloth their money could buy at the market, and held him to her breast. She kissed the top of his head repeatedly and cried tears of joy. "He is a fine baby, Manoah," she said.

"Yes, my love, of course he is. With such a strong, beautiful mother, how could he be anything else?"

"Come, you must hold him and give him your blessing."

"The priest will be here soon to bless him," Manoah replied. "It is better to wait for his blessing."

"No, Manoah. Never mind the priest. You give him your blessing."

Manoah looked at his wife and saw the determination on her face. With a sigh, he reached down and took the baby in his arms. He felt clumsy and fearful. He thought that his hands, long toughened and hardened in the forge, could not be gentle enough for this soft, little baby. But he was wrong. He lifted up the swaddled child and spoke with a loud singsong voice. "Oh God of Abraham, Isaac, and Israel, You alone have given this boy to us. You have instructed us to raise him as a special offering to You. Now we give him to You. You have instructed us through the Angel of the Lord, and we will follow Your directives. He will be a Nazirite all of his life. No razor shall come upon his head. No fruit of the vine shall touch his lips. No fermented drink shall he have. He will touch no dead thing. He will live as Your servant. Through him,

You will begin throwing off the yoke of the Philistines. Now, Sovereign Lord, your humble servants thank You. You have removed the scorn and disgrace heaped upon us by our brothers and sisters and have blessed us with a son from Your hand."

Zelponi watched Manoah as he spoke the prayer, her eyes glowing with new respect for her husband. He had never been a man who spoke eloquently as her father had first pointed out to her. Now, however, she heard the words come from his lips with ease. She knew those words had come from God. "Thank you, Manoah," she said. "You have spoken the words better than any priest could with their incense and beards."

"We must not despise the priests, my love," Manoah said softly, carefully handing the baby back to Zelponi. "They, too, have been set aside by God to serve His people."

"I do not see them serving God. It seems they are more determined to serve themselves. As it is, they say the law requires that they have the first fruits of everything. Some of them want the first, the last, and some of what is in between."

At that moment, the high priest, Korah, was escorted into the room by one of the servant girls. He was a tall man with a long, flowing, gray beard. A cream-colored tunic made of the finest linen flowed down to his feet and was held closed by a pure white sash twined and embroidered with mystic symbols. He had a short, cone-shaped turban on his head and wore tasseled slippers on his feet.

He had come from the city of Gibeon, one of the priestly cities. He had traveled a long distance to come here and was residing with the village priest in Zorah. He had been called for this purpose because of Manoah. The wealthiest men in the region could always count on the high priest himself to attend them when a special occasion arose. When Zelponi heard he was coming, she bluntly said that she thought he just wanted the blessing gift that was customarily given to the priest at such times, as the priests knew the gift would be substantial from someone like Manoah.

Manoah bowed his head slightly toward the priest as he entered the room.

"Is this the child?" Korah asked in his high-pitched voice.

"Yes, anointed one. This is our child," Manoah answered.

Manoah took the baby in his arms again and carefully handed him to Korah, who held him toward the ceiling. Zelponi cringed, fearful that the old man might drop her son.

"I have heard," said Korah, lowering the baby to cradle him somewhat clumsily in his arms, "of a visitation from an angel. Is this true?"

"Yes, esteemed one. It is true," replied Manoah.

"We will speak of that afterward."

Korah then handed the baby back to Manoah. He made some signs over the child with his right hand. He pulled a small leather pouch from under his tunic and put his thumb and index finger inside of it. When he pulled them out, they appeared to be coated with oil. He rubbed the fingers on his palms and wiped the palms together. Stepping back from Manoah, Korah raised his two hands toward heaven and spoke a prayer.

Although she heard it, Zelponi was not really listening, as it sounded like mumbling to her. She had grown to despise the priests, especially those who had come to her when she was barren and spoken their words of condemnation. Now she resented this man and his presumption of the right to speak a blessing over her son. Could his blessing be better than Manoah's? She pulled the covers up closer to her neck and watched with a scowl.

"And what is to be his name?" Korah asked when he had finished the prayer.

"His name will be Samson." Zelponi spoke quickly before Manoah could say anything.

"Samson? What kind of name is that?" asked Korah.

"It is the name we have chosen," Zelponi responded.

"Is this true?" Korah asked, looking at Manoah.

"If Zelponi says that his name is Samson, Samson is his name."

"Have you turned into sun worshippers too?" Korah asked with a sneer in his voice. "This is a sun name. Sun man or Sun hero. It is Egyptian foolishness. Why would you give a child of Dan such a name? Do you wish to be cursed? Would you have us worship cats and dogs like the Egyptians? We worship the one true God, not the sun or the moon. They will talk about you in the village, giving your son such a name."

"We are used to being talked about in the village," Zelponi said, not seeking to hide the scorn in her voice. "We worship the one true God and do not need you to tell us of the curses of Egypt. God Himself has told us that this child will be a blessing, and that he will help deliver the people from the hands of the Philistines. Samson is his name!" Zelponi lowered her voice almost to a whisper, but it seemed to have a hidden menace in it. "Anyway, a name does not always represent the character of a man, does it? Your name is Korah, is it not?"

"It is."

"Wasn't that the name of one who led the rebellion against Moses?" Zelponi asked, raising her eyebrows. "You are a Levite, as was he. I suppose being in the priestly tribe does not keep a person from making mistakes."

Manoah raised his eyebrows. He was not surprised at his wife's insult to Korah, but he was surprised at Zelponi's knowledge about the name. He knew that Perez had taught his daughter himself about the history of their people. What he did not know was that Perez himself had spent time with the priests as a young boy, learning the history of the people of Israel. Perez had never spoken of it. His conversations with Manoah had betrayed little in the way of reverence for the priests. Now Manoah wondered if something had happened to turn Perez away from the priests. Zelponi had said that Perez had been different since his wife died. Perhaps that was what brought about the change in him. His lack of reverence had been passed on to Zelponi and had only been increased by the actions of the priests when she was considered barren.

Korah's eyes grew wide at this insult to his name. He stepped back, almost staggering, and held out his hand with the palm facing toward Zelponi. Then he looked down as if awakening from a trance. He sighed and drew his hands into the folds of his tunic. He bowed toward Manoah and turned to leave. At the doorway, he stopped and turned back to face them. "His name is on your head. The priest of Zorah will be here in eight days to perform the circumcision. I will not return."

"Good," Zelponi said under her breath.

SAMSON: THE BOY

Manoah and Zelponi were loving parents. They treated their son as if he were the most important thing in the world to them. In fact, nothing was more important to them. The nursery room that they prepared for him was full of little toys that Manoah had lovingly carved out of algum wood. It also had paintings of little animals on the walls that Zelponi had drawn with coal and Manoah had painted with various colored pigments mixed with water. As Samson started to talk, they delighted in teaching him words and listening as he slowly began saying them.

When Samson was old enough to understand, Manoah and Zelponi told him about the visit from the Angel of the Lord and the vow they had taken on his behalf. When he was eight years old, Samson told his mother that he approved of the vow, and that he would keep it. By that time, his hair had become long, hanging down to his shoulders. Zelponi taught Samson how to braid his hair so it would not fly around and get in his eyes. At first he had trouble with it, and she delighted to do it for him. Every few days, she would take down his braids and wash his hair, soaking it with fragrant herbs. Then he would sit on a cushion before her chair, and she would slowly dry his hair and weave it into seven long braids. As she did this, she sang in a low, sweet voice a song she had sung to him since he was a baby, "My little boy, my little boy, Samson is my little boy. Rest your head softly now, my little boy." By the time she was done, Samson had leaned back against her knees and fallen asleep.

Zelponi loved to make rhymes for Samson and sing other songs to him. One of her favorites she made up when he shook at the sound of thunder as a tiny baby. She would cradle him in her arms, swaying from side to side and sing,

"Hush, little baby, don't you weep.
Momma's here with you, go to sleep.
Soon the clear sky the morning will bring.
So hush, little baby, while I sing.
Hush, little baby, don't you cry.
Momma's here with you, dry your eye.
Hush, little baby, Papa's here too.
So hush, little baby, he'll take care of you."

Samson ran through the grain fields with his arms stretched out beside him like the wings of a bird, crying out in a loud voice, "Aww, aww, aww! Look, father, I am an eagle, flying down to eat your grain!"

"I never saw an eagle eating grain," Manoah replied, laughing. "Oh no, my son, they eat little boys, especially those with wings. They like to pick the wings clean with their sharp beaks. You better watch out for them."

"I am not afraid of any eagle. Let him come down. I will jump on his back and ride him up into the sky. Aww, aww, aww!"

"Would you not rather be a snake that slithers along the ground and hides from his enemies? The snake is the true symbol for our tribe, the tribe of Dan."

Samson stopped running and walked over to his father. He often came with his father to the fields. He would run and play while his father sat on a wooden stool and watched.

"The priest told me it is also the eagle," he said. "He said that when we came out of Egypt, the symbol for the eagle flew over the tribes of Dan, Asher, and Naphtali, so we can claim the eagle also."

"Well, sometimes the priests say what they think to be true, but that does not make it so. My father told me the symbol of our tribe was the snake."

"The priests told me that the name of our tribe represents judgment. The judgment of God was upon the snake in the garden. Our father, Israel, said that justice would come through Dan, and we would be like a snake by the roadside."

"Yes, that is all true, I suppose," Manoah mused. "You will know much more than me about such things as you grow older, Son."

"Why do I have to listen to the priests, father? Why must they come every week to the house to give me instructions? They do not do that with other boys from the village and sometimes they are so boring." Samson changed his voice to a sing song monotone and with a deep scowl on his face he mimicked the voice of one of the priests, "Our Father Abraham was the founder of the nation of Israel. He had a son named Issac, who had two sons, Jacob and Esau. Jacob's name was changed to Israel by God Himself, and his twelve sons became the tribes of Israel. There was Reuben, Simeon, Levi, Judah, Dan, Naphtali, Gad, Asher, Issachar, Zebulun, Joseph and Benjamin. These are the twelve sons of Jacob and the twelve tribes of Israel, of which we, the tribe of Dan are one."

Manoah laughed at Samson's imitation of the priest.

"I pay them to instruct you, Son. I am afraid that you are not like other boys. God has selected you to serve Him. You cannot serve God if you do not know His law and His ways."

"But why did He choose me, and why can't I cut my hair?" After telling his mother that he would keep the Nazirite vow, Samson wondered about the vow and why he should keep it.

"I do not know why, Son. I only know what God has told us. Your mother and I made a vow before God that we would raise you as a Nazirite. That is why I pay the priests to teach you the Nazirite way so you, too, can commit yourself to God. You told your mother you would keep the vow, and that has made us both very happy."

"I do not understand much of what the priests tell me, father. They taught me why we celebrate the Passover and the other festivals, but the rest seems very hard. Don't do this, don't do that."

"God gave us the law to guide us, Son. We have to decide each day how to follow it. The priests are just trying to help us."

"Mother does not think so. She hates the priests."

"I do not think she hates them. That would be a sin. She just thinks they are not always right. And she is probably correct. The priests are also men, like us. They make mistakes too."

"Men like us? Am I a man now, father?"

"Well, not quite yet. Some of the priests say that when you have passed thirteen years we call you a man. Others say it should be older. I do not know. Do you think you are a man already?"

"I don't know. I like to play. I don't see any men playing."

"No, but perhaps we should. Playing is a good thing. Come on, eagle. I am an eagle too!"

Manoah got up from his stool and ran through the fields, his arms stretched out to his sides. "Aww, aww, aww! I am king of the eagles," he cried out.

"Aww, aww, aww! I am the son of the king," Samson responded.

A loud metallic tapping sound came from the direction of their house.

"That is Mother hitting the cook pot," Samson yelled. "Supper is ready. Come on, King Eagle, I will race you to the house!"

Together they ran down the road, Manoah huffing and puffing behind the young boy.

Zelponi stood at the front door of the house with a small round cook pot in her hands and a wooden spoon. As she had done for her father and Manoah at the forge when meals were ready, she called her husband and son from the fields by standing at the front door with a wooden spoon and a small cook pot in her hands and hitting the bottom of the pot rhythmically with the spoon. *Tap-tap-tap. Tap-tap-tap. Tap-tap-tap-tap-tap-tap-tap.* She repeated this sequence twice and then waited for her two men to appear.

"Here we are, Mother. Two hungry eagles come back to the nest to eat," called Samson as they approached the house.

"Eagles? I don't have any food for eagles," Zelponi responded. "They eat rats and mice and other birds. You don't want any of that, do you?"

"Yes, yes, let's have some rat stew and some mouse pie!" Samson shouted eagerly, jumping up and down and clapping his hands together. He amused himself very much by this and broke into peals of laughter.

Manoah laughed, too, and said in a whiny voice, "Aww, aww, aww! Give us some rat stew."

"Aww, aww, aww! Yes, a big bowl of rat stew," Samson echoed, holding his face toward Zelponi and moving his mouth like the beak of a bird.

"You two may have the brains of birds, but you still have to come into the house and wash yourselves," Zelponi said, turning to walk into the house. "We are having plain roasted vegetables and a small bit of lamb. No rat stew today."

Samson looked up at his father. "Aw, no rat stew, King Eagle. We will just have to eat the moldy vegetables. Can't we at least have the lamb raw with blood and tear it with our beaks?"

"No," Manoah sighed. "I guess we will just have to eat what Queen Eagle puts on the table for us. Now go and wash."

Samson grew rapidly, and as he grew, the visits of the priests to the house declined and gradually stopped. Like his mother, Samson had no taste for their company. He had learned to read from the scrolls of Scripture and to copy down the words on the blank scrolls the priests gave him. He enjoyed the writing part, especially writing his name at the bottom of each scroll. He delighted in shaping the letters in large sweeping form and often wrote them backwards. When he wrote his name, he always wrote the first and middle letters backwards. The priests, of course, had corrected him but to no avail.

"I have learned the Ten Commandments and the history of our people," he told his mother and father. "What else do I need to learn? How far I can walk on the Sabbath or how to tell if a spot on my skin is infectious or not? Let the priests know all of that. It is their job."

Zelponi and Manoah said nothing in response.

When Samson reached the age of fifteen, the priest of Zorah declared that he was a man. He had wanted to make the declaration two years earlier, but Zelponi had said no. She did not think that Samson was ready yet, and after she and Manoah discussed it, they had informed the priest that they would wait until Samson was fifteen.

A great feast was held, and the entire village was invited to the house of his father to celebrate. Tables were set out in the back of the house, covered by white linen. Awnings, set on poles, covered the tables to keep out the sun. Servants brought out streams of food. There were wheat cakes with honey, young lamb cooked over an open flame, roasted quail in a bed of leeks and garlic, melons, figs, dates, and pomegranates.

Although Samson and his mother could drink no wine and eat no grapes, they were there for their guests. Manoah was not under such a rule, so he drank with the guests and got quite lively, dancing to the tune of the musicians he had hired to celebrate his son's manhood. Samson danced also, a wild and energetic run around the tables. He gave his eagle cry and swooped past the ladies, who shrieked in fake horror. Some of his friends from the village joined in his mad dance.

Zelponi sat apart from it all, quietly eating her food and drinking only water spiced with cloves and honey. She had no friends in the village. As they had once scorned her, she now scorned them and made no attempt to hide it. She almost resented them coming to her house, but, for her son's sake, she bore it, smiling as best she could at the men and ladies who walked past to pay their respects to the richest woman for miles around. She knew they came for the food and the manhood gift that would be given to every guest.

"Come, Mother, won't you dance too?" Samson asked, grabbing her hands and pulling her to her feet.

"No, don't be foolish. It is not seemly for a forty-year-old woman to be dancing."

"Who said so?" Samson grabbed her around the waist and whirled her up in the air in a circle.

"Samson! Put me down, you rascal. I will get all dizzy!"

He lifted her in his arms and ran completely around the huge circle of tables, shrieking at the top of his lungs, "Aww, aww, aww!. The eagle prince and his mother, Queen Eagle, greet you!"

"Samson, put me down!" she cried, although she was laughing so hard tears were in her eyes.

Finally, he brought her back to her chair and set her down in front of it. "Did you like the ride, Mother?" he laughed.

"How did you lift me up that way, just a young boy like you? I am no feather on the eagle's back, you know. I'm afraid I look more like a blacksmith's wife every day. Wide around the middle."

"You were light as a feather to me."

Manoah walked up behind them, a curious look on his face. "You have grown very strong, my son," he said.

"I know, Father. I felt like picking Mother up, and I just did it. I didn't know I could until I did."

"The priests and Judge Abdon were quite amazed. You should have seen the look on their faces. They had never seen a young eagle like you before."

"Did they think the son of a blacksmith would be a weakling? Ha! Wait until I grow older. Then I will show them strength."

"Be careful, my son," murmured Manoah. "Do not let pride overtake you. If you are strong, it is a strength that comes from God who set you apart for His purposes."

Samson pointed to a chair next to Zelponi. "Sit down a moment, Father." Samson sat down across from his parents. He looked at them and then down at his hands and spoke slowly. "You have been telling me since I was a young child about God choosing me and the vow you took for me. A vow I took myself when I was younger. But I really don't understand about the angel. The priests admonished me when I spoke of it, so I didn't speak of it any longer to them."

"I told you they were fools!" Zelponi burst out.

"I do not think they are fools, Mother. They just don't understand. They asked me, 'When did an Angel of the Lord God appear to anyone in Israel since the days of Joshua?' What they have not seen for themselves, they find hard to believe. Father, didn't you also doubt until you saw and heard Him for yourself?'

"Yes. Yes, Son, I did," answered Manoah. "To speak the truth, I doubted until I saw Him ascend to heaven in the flame. At first, I was resentful and jealous that He came to your mother and not to me. I thought perhaps this was some stranger trying to take advantage of your mother's innocence. Then when He stepped into the fire, I knew your mother and I had seen God Himself. He had come to us just as He appeared to Joshua and to Moses. Yes, the priests doubted. Perhaps they doubted my sanity, but they said that if He did go up in the flame, surely it must have been the Angel of the Lord. Of course, that is just a name they use when God, whose name we cannot say, walks here among men. I was even more sure when I thought about it afterward. When I asked His name, He said it was beyond my ability to understand. Who else has a name like that except the one who told Moses His name was simply I Am? When I asked Him if He was the angel who had appeared to your mother, He responded, 'I am.' I did not realize what that meant at the time, but I do now."

"But how does that help me, Father? What am I supposed to do? You told me that you do not want me to be a blacksmith or a farmer. So what do I do?"

"God has blessed us with great wealth, my son. You can do whatever your heart desires. I do not want to tell you what to do. Perhaps you should be a soldier. As small as the army of Israel has become, every village and city has its soldiers to protect us all and its judges to rule us. Maybe you will be appointed a judge. Who can say? You must seek the will of God. Every man must find that for himself. What I tell you may not be what God wants, so you must wait for Him to tell you."

"But how will He tell me? Will He come again as an angel?"

"I do not know, Son."

"You will know when He tells you, Samson," Zelponi said. "He will speak to you in some way. He speaks to us in the wind and in the trees and in the people around us. His voice is everywhere."

"I have never heard you speak of the Lord God that way, Mother. You always talk so badly about the priests."

"I have little respect for the priests, Samson, that is true. But that does not mean I do not believe and love the Lord God. I know we do not honor all of the feasts or the festivals, but what is important is that we honor God in our hearts. Your father and I feel that God had the angel of barrenness pass over us, so how could I not believe in Him? It was He who gave you to me and to your father. And I am grateful for that gift every day. You have been such a joy to our lives. I cannot imagine what life would have been without you." Tears filled Zelponi's eyes.

Samson got up, bent over to hug her, and patted the back of her head. "I am the one who is blessed, Mother. You and Father have been like God to me. Everything I could ever want you have given me. I just hope I won't ever be a disappointment to you."

"You could never be that, my son. Never. Now go, and sit with your friends."

Samson walked off to join a group of young people who were playing tambourines and dancing. He joined them and was soon dancing around the tables again.

"Your son is a fine young man, Manoah," Zelponi said.

"Yes, my love, he is. He is like his mother, strong and beautiful."

"Phhh. You talk nonsense sometimes."

"No, my darling, no, I do not. Now it is time to present the man gift." Manoah stood and walked to the edge of the tables where the guests were seated. "My dear friends." He held up his hands to get their attention. "It is time for the presentation of Samson's gift for manhood."

The guests began cheering and calling Samson's name.

"Come here, my boy," Manoah said.

Samson walked slowly to his father's side. He had not been told about this part of the ceremony and wondered what his father had in store for him. Manoah gestured again for the guests to be silent.

"Samson," he said. "Today is your first day of manhood. The priests have examined you and found you ready. I have a special gift to mark this great occasion. Tolas, bring the gift."

Tolas was a blacksmith who had managed the forge since Manoah's retirement. He came forward now with a large object wrapped in linen and tied with scarlet yarn. He handed it to Manoah.

"Samson, I am sorry that your grandfather is not here for this day. Perez was a great blacksmith. He taught me everything I know. He would have been very proud to see this day and his fine grandson. In his honor, I present you with this gift to mark your passage into manhood. It is a gift I have hammered out with my own hands."

Samson took the large package from his father, snapped the yarn, and pulled off the linen covering. Beneath it was a large shield made of hammered gold, polished like the finest mirror. It was a full body shield like those used among the Philistines, measuring five feet in length and almost three feet in width. It was a magnificent piece of work with soaring eagles etched around the edge. At the top in bold letters was inscribed "Samson" with the first and middle letters etched backwards, just as he had written it since he was a small boy. At the bottom was a large coiled snake. Samson held the shield high in the air, his face beaming with pride, as the crowd of guests all shouted, "Samson, the man!"

SAMSON: THE MAN

When Samson was twenty-seven years old, the elders of the tribe of Dan came to visit him. The oldest, the governor of Ekron, spoke for them as they sat in the front room of Manoah's house. "Samson, we have come on behalf of the tribesmen of Dan and the people of Israel. We wish to ask you to consider being a judge of Israel."

"Me?" Samson asked. "Why choose me?"

"It has not gone unnoticed by us that you are a man of strength and courage. That is what we need to lead us should the Philistines arise against us. You were trained by the priests when you were a boy, and so you should know the basics of the law. That in itself qualifies you above any of the other men your age in the entire region."

"I am not even sure what a judge is expected to do. I have only met one of them, Abdon, who came to my manhood ceremony. I never even spoke to him about what a judge was or what he did."

"The blessed Abdon is dead. As to what a judge does, it is nothing large unless circumstances dictate otherwise. A judge is expected to lead us in any military campaigns that may arise. Sometimes he is called on to settle disputes, although the priests handle that pretty well without the judges."

"I am not a soldier. I know nothing about leading an army."

"As you know, we have no formal army. Every tribe of Israel is expected to have able men ready at any time to fight our enemies. In the times of Moses and Joshua, the men were listed and counted. Now it is much more informal, as the tribes have spread across the land. Nobody today knows how many men we could call together if we needed them. That would be one of the tasks of a judge, to recruit soldiers when the time came."

"I do not think you have the right man. I have nothing against the Philistines. I have journeyed to their lands with my father at times, and I see no harm in them. Many of them seem just like us except they worship false gods. They are just blind about that. They cannot see, and maybe we have not done anything to show them the one true God."

"That is precisely another reason why you would serve well in this position. You know the enemy. You have been in their cities and have seen their ways. What better person to lead us against them than one who knows them?"

"Oh, so I am to be not just a judge, but also a spying judge."

"There is no dishonor in spying. Moses sent spies into this land before the people of Israel were to enter it. Joshua, too, sent out spies. It is a good military tactic to know the enemy."

"Suppose I don't want to fight them? I see no need for it."

"Neither do we, my boy. We have no desire to engage them in battle. However, we would be negligent in our duty if we were not prepared to do so if the need arises, as I said."

Manoah, who had been sitting quietly at Samson's side during this conversation, now spoke. "Do not be hasty in saying no, my son. It may be that this is God's will for you. Remember the prophecy given to your mother and me before your birth. God may well plan to use you to guard Israel against the Philistines. Although we have had only minor skirmishes with them for many years, they are an ambitious people. Their cities grow rapidly, and they have expanded their borders right up to our doorsteps. The people of Dan have had to leave many of the areas on the coast that we love because of the Philistines. I, too, see no reason to fight them, but if a fight should come, we must be prepared. Seek the Lord about this, and do not give your answer until you are sure it is what He wants."

"Your father gives good counsel, Samson," the governor said. "You may have time to think. Call for us when you have an answer."

The elders arose as one and left the house. Samson turned to his mother, who had sat quietly across the room from the men. She felt that this was not an issue for her involvement.

"What about you, Mother? What do you say?"

Zelponi stood and crossed the room. With a sigh, she reached up and cupped her son's face in her hands. "God must be exalted in your life, my son. That is all I know. The Angel of the Lord spoke to your father and me those many years ago. He said that God would begin the deliverance of Israel from the hands of the Philistines through you. What does that mean? We are still not sure to this day. I only know that what the Lord God Himself told us will come to pass. He is not a man that He should lie. But as your father said, it is you who must find out what it means. If it is to be a judge, so be it. The Lord be glorified."

"Yes, Mother."

Samson left the house and walked down the path in the direction of the sea. Although it was many miles away, he loved to just walk toward it and sense its presence over the hills. His father and mother had taken him to the seaside many times when he was younger to watch the waves roll in and then wash back out. He loved it especially when a storm arose and the water thrashed and beat against the shore.

The people of Dan loved to go out on the sea. Many of Samson's friends had boarded ships for other lands to seek their fortunes. Now he looked in the direction of the sea, feeling as if a large wave were washing over him. He did not like the idea of being a judge, and especially not a spy. However, what if this was what God wanted from him?

Samson did not consider himself a man of God. Although he believed what his parents had told him about the visitation from God, he was not sure what it meant for him, or even if it meant anything at all. He had lived a pampered life and was quite comfortable in it. His father and mother gave him everything he asked for.

Samson sighed deeply and turned back toward the house. God would have to show him.

Several days after the visit of the elders, Samson told Manoah and Zelponi that he had decided to accept the offer from the elders and become a judge.

"Samson the judge!" Manoah exclaimed. "My son, a judge of Israel. May God be praised!"

"We are proud of you, Son," Zelponi said. "We are sure that you are doing what God would have you do."

"I am not so sure, Mother. But last night I had a feeling that God was talking to me. I heard no voice and saw no angel, but something inside of me would not be still. When I walked outside and looked up at the stars, I became quite sure that I must be a judge. I don't want to be, but can I ignore what the Angel of the Lord said to you when I feel so strongly that this is what He was talking about? I cannot, even though I would like to run away and forget I ever heard of judges."

"You cannot run away from God, my son," Zelponi responded. "No matter where you go, He will find you."

Within a week, Samson was sent to a training camp for local soldiers from the tribe of Dan. He spent two months there, talking to the commanders and other officers. He was poorly versed in sword fighting despite the fact that his father produced the best forged swords in the country, so he had to go through the same rigorous course as other young men who had been chosen from their families.

In trial fights with the young recruits, nobody wanted Samson as an opponent. He was an imposing figure, and few men matched him in stature. Most of the other men were little more than older boys, most of them between fifteen and seventeen years old. However, Samson restrained himself and helped the younger men, as together they learned the methods of combat.

Samson also made commitments to the commander to supply arms for the men from his father's forge. Each recruit would be guaranteed his own sword and shield. In the years since settling the land, the Israelites had not spent much time preparing for war. They had been too busy farming and building their cities. The peace that had followed Joshua's conquest of the land had lulled them into complacence. Unlike the

Philistines, who were always preparing for war, the Israelites had spent more of their time and money on buying farm implements.

When Samson returned home from his training, his parents greeted him with great joy.

"Well, Son, what do you plan to do now as the newest judge of Israel?" Manoah asked.

"I intend to start my career as a judge with a visit to the Philistines. Perhaps the Spirit of God is sending me. I will travel tomorrow down to Timnah. You have many trading partners there, Father. I will go on your behalf."

"Just be careful, my son. You must always be on your guard, just as I was when I went the first time with my friend Micah. Watch everyone, and trust nobody there."

"Yes, Father."

The next day, Samson set out on his journey. Although his father had horse carts and even two chariots, he preferred to ride a black stallion his father had given him some years before. It was a spirited animal, and few people could control him except Samson. His name was Thunder. Samson also took another horse with him loaded down with sample swords, shields, and spears.

When Samson reached Timnah, he hired a room at a wayside inn on the road leading into the city. On his first day, he went to visit some of the arms merchants who had shops there. He introduced himself as the son of Manoah, the producer of fine weapons.

The largest shop owner, whose name was Booleon, welcomed him with great enthusiasm. "Welcome, son of Manoah! Your father is the finest producer of swords and lances in the land. It has been many years since he visited us. How is he? Does he well?"

"Yes, my father is very well. He does not travel much anymore. He has many agents who travel for him. Now he has asked me to come down and meet his customers. I suppose he hopes that some day I will take over his business, even though I am no blacksmith."

"Your father has taught his other blacksmiths their art well. His forge produces the finest weapons I have ever seen. I assure you that as long as they do so, he will have a regular customer in me. Our people cannot get enough of good weapons. If they don't use them in war, at least they love to hang them on their walls and admire them."

"Well, I think the forge will continue to produce well for you. My father has trained a score of blacksmiths there, and they work every day to supply all that you need. If you have any special needs or requests, I can take them back to him personally."

"We can talk of that later. For tonight, come and dine with me. I will invite some of the other merchants, and we will have a great feast to celebrate the son of Manoah coming to visit us."

"It would be a pleasure to eat with you.'

"Then come to the tavern of the Red Boar at the dinner hour. They have splendid food and drink."

"I will be there."

As evening approached, Samson dressed in his finest linen tunic with gold braids around the hem and made his way to the tavern of the Red Boar, a large eating-place near the outskirts of the town that stood on the main road. The walls outside were lined with long torches in brackets. A huge banner with an emblem shaped like a large boar embroidered in red thread hung down over the doorway.

Samson entered the building and was immediately greeted by a loud cheer from Booleon, who stood at the doorway to greet him. "Hail to Samson, son of Manoah, the armor maker!"

There were cheers around the room, and men came up to him and greeted him warmly, hitting him on the shoulder and laughing. Booleon led him to a large table where he was introduced to some of the local leaders of the Philistines.

"This is Tiburon, the governor of Timnah," Booleon said.

"How do you do, my boy? It is a pleasure to meet you."

"The pleasure is mine, Governor," replied Samson.

"And this, Samson, is Phicol," Booleon continued around the table. "Phicol is the commander of the armed forces for the Philistine army here in Timnah."

Phicol stood up from where he was seated. He was a tall man, half a head taller than Samson, with a large barrel chest and a booming voice. He wore a long mustache and a neatly trimmed short beard. He held out his right arm to Samson in the traditional greeting of peace. "Hail, Samson. I am proud to meet you. Your father has sent me some of the finest weapons I own. It is many years since I have seen him personally, but it is a great pleasure to meet his son."

"Hail to you, Commander Phicol. I am happy to hear that my father has provided well for you. I am sure he will continue to do so."

Samson sat down in the chair that had been set for him at the head of the table. Others were introduced, and he greeted them all warmly. Samson had never felt so important in his life. He had known that his father was held in high esteem for the weapons he produced, but he had not been prepared for this special greeting from the Philistines. It made him more certain that they were not enemies to his people. Why would they greet their enemy in this manner? They were no different than the people of Israel. They just wanted to live their lives in peace. Samson smiled, glad he had come.

Soon platters of food were brought out from the kitchen. The specialty of the tavern was, of course, roasted wild boar cooked slowly over a flame in a pit behind the building. Samson hesitated about eating this. He knew his people had many dietary restrictions, and that he was forbidden to eat certain foods, but he did not wish to insult his hosts. He tasted all of the food and found it delicious. He would not, however, break the vow he had taken, so he drank no wine or fermented drink. He asked for water and refused to drink anything else.

"No wine, Samson?" Booleon asked. "We have some of the finest wine in the region here. You are missing a great treat not to taste it."

"I am sorry, Booleon, but wine is one thing that has never agreed with my stomach. I must limit myself to water or I will be spending too much time out back relieving myself later on. It would be a shame to let all of this fine food come back up because of a little wine."

"As you please, my friend. Yes, it is a shame to have a tender stomach when it comes to drink. Drinking is one of our great pleasures here. We spend a lot of time doing it and send out buyers to find the best of wines and other spirits."

As the evening wore on, Samson was introduced to other people who had come to the feast. The most striking of these was a beautiful young girl named Merari, the daughter of Booleon. Samson invited her to sit by him. She said that she was greatly honored to do so. She had long auburn hair that hung down over her shoulders in braids, much like the braids of his own hair. Samson was stuck immediately by her beauty.

Samson had never known a woman physically, in spite of his age. His mother and father had admonished him, as had the priests, about loose morals when it came to women. There were many young women where he lived. Most of them worked in the fields and lived at home with their parents. Some were attractive and some smart, but none had ever attracted Samson like Merari. She sat by him all evening, smiling and laughing at the jests he made. Samson loved to make jests, recite poetry, and create riddles.

"Which of the stars are the most important ones, Merari?" he asked.

"I do not know, Samson. Which ones?"

"All of the stars there in those beautiful eyes of course," he said, pointing to her eyes.

"Oh Samson," Merari giggled. "You are so smart and funny. You are not like the Philistine men. They are all very serious, always talking about either war or weapons or wine. I like you."

"I like you, too, Merari."

In the days to come, Samson spent many hours with Merari. He hired a chariot to take her out riding along the highway that led away from the city toward the coastal area near the cities of Ashkelon and Gaza. Merari was a most willing companion, and her father delighted in the relationship that developed between her and Samson. He knew full well that Samson's father had vast wealth. Having his daughter linked with such a family could only do him good. His own wife, who had died giving birth to Merari's younger sister a year after Merari was born, had been a woman of Israel. However, Booleon did not talk of this much, as he feared the Philistine leaders and their suspicions of anyone connected to the Israelites. Most of them had known nothing about his wife or where she came from, and he preferred to keep it that way.

Finally, the day came when Samson planned to return home. He had spoken to Merari of the affection he had developed for her and asked her if she might be willing to marry him. He would not, of course, marry her unless her father agreed and arranged the matter according to the laws of the Philistines. Merari would not say she was willing, but neither did she say she was opposed to the idea. She liked to tease Samson and pretend she did not care for him. Then he would tease her back, and they would laugh. She really had developed a deep affection for him and did not object at all to the idea of marrying him. However, she did not want to seem too anxious, so she acted indifferent to the idea.

"I might marry you if you act properly," she said with a twinkle in her eye.

"What do I have to do to act properly? Bring you silver and gold?"

"That would certainly be a proper beginning." Merari laughed loudly. "Yes, Samson, my big, brave man. That would be a good start."

Samson laughed at this too and left her to pack his few belongings and start the journey home.

Samson was proud of himself. He had written up many orders for weapons from the forge and signed some contracts with new purchasers who had not done business with his father before. He also had met all of the military commanders and felt that he had gained their trust. He knew how many men were in the local military branch, loosely organized as it was, and that they had a vast store of weapons. Commander Phicol had told him this and cautioned him to be careful with whom he shared this information. Samson had not taken the admonishment as a threat, even though Phicol had meant it that way, as he had little tolerance for spies. He had killed many a suspected spy in his time. He would not hesitate to kill Samson if the need arose.

MERARI: THE WIFE

When Samson returned home, his mother and father greeted him warmly. It had been the first time he had been away from home, and they had missed him greatly. Without Samson there, they had lost interest in all the things around them. For so many years, they had lived their lives to please their son. They had no other children, so all of their love was directed toward him. They had even neglected their love for each other in their focus on Samson, so when he was gone, they hardly knew what to say to each other. When he returned, the light came back into their eyes, and they rejoiced and held a feast to celebrate his homecoming. He had only been gone for a month, but it seemed like years to them.

"Father and Mother, I am home!" he shouted as he swept into the house. "Your son has returned alive from among the Philistines. They have not killed me yet!"

Zelponi ran to greet her son from the kitchen, where she had been baking bread. Although she had many servants now, like Manoah she could not resist working. Without work she felt useless.

"Oh my son, my son!" she exclaimed as he hugged and lifted her in the air, twirling her around the room.

"Put me down, Samson. I am too old for that. You will make me dizzy!"

"A little dizziness won't hurt you, Mother. You are not allowed to get dizzy from wine, so let me make you dizzy another way."

"You young rascal. Put me down."

Finally, he did and then hugged and kissed her more. "I am glad to be home, Mother, although I had a wonderful time in Timnah."

"Well, you can tell us all about it when we eat supper. Your father will be back from the forge soon and will want to hear everything."

"The forge? What is he doing there? He hardly ever goes there anymore."

"He has hired and is training three new blacksmith apprentices. He said he wanted to oversee the training himself this time. He was quite certain that your journey would bring more business to the forge, and he wanted to be prepared."

"He has always been a good businessman, and he was right. I have a whole list of new orders for swords, shields, and spears. It will keep them busy for months to come."

"You go and wash, and I will sound the pot for him to come and eat." True to her tradition as always, Zelponi went to the front of the house with the small pot and wooden spoon and did her *tap-tap-tap. Tap-tap-tap. Tap-tap-tap-tap-tap-tap-tap.* Manoah would soon be there.

When Manoah entered the house, Samson rushed and grabbed him off his feet as he had done with his mother. Lifting him up high, Samson laughed and shouted, "Your boy is home!"

Manoah laughed until tears ran from his eyes, and Samson finally put him down. "It is so wonderful having you back, my son. You cannot imagine how much your mother and I have missed you. Every day at this time we have watched the road, hoping to see you riding back home."

"I am here now, Father, and I have so much to tell you!"

"Good. Just let me wash my hands, and you can tell us everything as we eat."

The meal was a joyous one for the most part as Samson told of all the people he had met. He proudly pulled from his tunic a large sheaf of parchment, on which he had written names and orders for armor.

"Brand-new customers, Father! They were all talking about you and the fine work that comes from your shop. They don't call it a forge or a blacksmith shop. They call it an armory and said that yours is the finest in the land of Canaan! They have sent gold on deposit for every order."

With that, Samson pulled a large pouch that had been hanging from his belt and spilled its contents out on the table. Gold, bronze, and silver coins rolled across the table toward his father, who laughed and scooped them up.

"So your first trip has been a great success, eh, my son?"

"Imagine, Father. They were so anxious that I sold all of my samples in a single day! They could not wait to place their orders! The word of Phicol the commander was enough to convince anyone who was interested."

"Yes, I have a long-standing relationship with Phicol. He is a shrewd man, and you must be careful of him. He speaks well of us because he knows I give him a better price for the recommendations that he makes. His word is law in that city. He is a good customer, but you would do well to stay away from him."

"He seemed harmless enough to me."

"Yes. Many of the Philistines seem harmless, but still they push their territory farther north every year. Some say they rule over us. We certainly depend on them to support our business. I am not an alarmist like the priests, but we must be on guard at all times."

"That doesn't sound like you, Father. You have always embraced them as tradesmen and customers."

"I suppose it is different when my son is among them. You are young and excitable, Samson. A man like Phicol can be very dangerous to a young man from the little tribe of Dan."

"I am not afraid of him. He couldn't hurt me."

"Don't be too sure of yourself, my son. Pride is a terrible thing. It can cause the strongest man to stumble and be brought down."

"Anyway, that is enough of that talk," said Zelponi. "Tell us what else you saw and did."

"I met a girl, Mother."

"A girl? What kind of girl?"

"A wonderful girl. She is beautiful and smart and funny. I would like for Father to come down and negotiate the bride price for her and get her to be my wife."

"A wife? My son, this is the first trip you have made and already you find a wife?" Zelponi asked. "That is madness. What do you know about this girl?'

"Her father is Booleon, another of father's customers. He has the largest weapons store in the city, and his daughter is Merari. She is half Israeli. Her mother was a Hebrew. She is a wonderful girl and is just right for me. I want to marry her."

Manoah had been silent all during this discussion, but now he spoke. "Samson, my son, is there no woman here among our own brethren you can marry? Must you marry a Philistine woman?"

"I told you that she is half Hebrew."

"That will mean little to our people. They will just think of her as a Philistine with a father who purchases arms for our enemies."

"How can you say that, Father? You sell more arms to them than Booleon ever will!"

"Yes, but I am not a Philistine."

"I know that, but this is the girl for me. I want you to get her for me."

"Son, we have never refused you anything that you asked of us. We will not refuse this if you are certain that this is from God. That should be the only thing that is important to you. Remember when we talked of your becoming a judge? We said you had to wait, and that God would tell you, and He did. Has He also told you about this marriage?"

"I think so, Father. From the moment I saw Merari I wanted her."

"There are many things we might want that are contrary to the will of God, Samson. You are a young man and have never known a woman. It is most natural for you to long to have a wife and the love that comes from her and the other things as well. However, once you make the choice, it is forever. When I chose your mother, I knew that nothing in the world would ever make me regret my decision. Nothing has. I love her more as the years pass, and no power on this earth will change that. If you feel and act that same way toward this girl, you will be fine. But if you have doubts about it, you should wait."

"I have no doubts, Father."

"Then we will go to Timnah." Manoah looked at his wife. She nodded and bowed her head in a silent prayer.

For the next several days, the house of Manoah was in a feverish state of preparation. A new dress was made for Zelponi of the finest material from the East. Manoah had a new tunic and robe sewn for Samson and for himself. They were cream-colored and fringed with purple borders. Samson was fitted for a new pair of boots made from soft calf leather. They were white and trimmed with strips of gold forged in Manoah's shop. They packed enough clothes to stay for a month into their finest cart, which was open in the front but covered with skins in the rear to provide a haven from the weather for Zelponi. Two fine white stallions would pull the carriage, and Samson would ride beside on Thunder.

Within two weeks, they were ready for the journey and set out on the road to Timnah.

A few miles from Timnah was a large grove of grapevines. As they approached it, Zelponi called out to Samson, who pulled his horse up to the carriage.

"Yes, Mother?"

"There is a vineyard here, my son. Remember your vow. We must not pass through such a place. We do not want to risk even touching the fruits on the vines."

"I did not when I came before. I went through the hills there to the East. But the cart will not make it on that road. You can go on the road off to the west that goes around the groves. I will meet you in the city."

Samson started off toward the hills. Soon he was among them, riding up the steep side of the hills and then down the other side to the outskirts of the city.

As Samson came through a narrow pass, he saw a strange sight before him. A lion had caught a young oryx and was crouched down, feeding on the carcass. As Samson approached, the lion lifted its head and roared. Samson's horse reared up in fear. Samson dismounted and slowly approached the lion. The animal roared again, hesitant to leave its prey.

"Who are you, Mr. Lion?" Samson laughed. "That looks like a nice meal you are having there."

As he approached the beast, it suddenly sprang up toward him, its huge jaws open wide. Samson stood his ground, and as the lion reached him, he grabbed it by the jaws and pulled. To his own astonishment, the animal came apart in his hands, torn in two like a thin sheet of parchment.

Samson stood over the body in wonder. He had never experienced such a thing. He had known his strength was considerable from when he was a child, but now this huge animal rendered as if it were nothing. He dropped the pieces of the beast and walked on, leading his horse to a nearby stream where he washed off the blood that had splattered on his hands and arms. He was amazed and glad it did not get on his clothes at all. Samson decided to say nothing of this to his parents. His mother would just worry about him.

In Timnah, Samson and his father went to the house of Booleon after establishing Zelponi at the best inn the city had to offer. Booleon did not seem at all surprised to see them.

"I have been wondering when our young Samson would return," he said. "Merari has been most anxious to see you again."

"And I to see her," Samson replied.

"We have come on a serious matter, Booleon," Manoah said. "Samson wishes to marry your daughter."

"I had hoped that was the purpose of your visit," Booleon replied. "When Samson visited us, he spent a lot of time with Merari, and she became very fond of him. When I asked her if she would marry him, she said yes. I had hoped that what I suspected about them was true, that they loved each other."

"You know the gravity of such a marriage between an Israelite and a Philistine, Booleon. It is not something we should take lightly," Manoah said.

"No, my dear man, it is not. I do not take it lightly. You are highly respected here as a supplier of the finest arms in the country. However, we are still considered ancient enemies. Samson has no doubt told you that Merari is half Hebrew. I do not speak of that among my people, as they frown on mixed marriages. And they will frown on this one, no doubt. However, they will not frown for long. As Samson proves himself a friend to the Philistines, they will be proud to embrace him."

"I certainly hope so, Booleon. I certainly hope so."

For the next few days, arrangements were made for the marriage. The Philistine ruling council gave their assent on the recommendation of Commander Phicol. A contract was drawn up and signed by the two families. The food and drink for the feast was ordered, and the Red Boar Inn was reserved as a marriage hall.

Manoah and Zelponi agonized over this. They had so looked forward to their son marrying a woman from his own people. Then they could have a proper marriage ceremony under the traditions of Israel. Now they followed the traditions of the Philistines instead, which was to feast and drink for a full week. It was expected to be an orgy of drinking. The marriage itself would take place on the first day of the feast. Manoah and Zelponi would leave to go back to their home before the rest of the revelry began.

The date of the wedding was set for two months later. In the meantime, Manoah and Zelponi would return home with Samson. They wondered how they would tell their neighbors about all of this. But they did not have to worry, as the neighbors already knew. Word had spread from the servants in Manoah's house to the servants in other houses.

When they returned home, the priest of Zorah was there to greet them within a few hours. He asked about the marriage, and if it was indeed true that a judge of Israel was to take a Philistine bride. Manoah's answer did not please him.

"I do not care if she is part Hebrew," the priest responded. "Her father is a Philistine and, to make it worse, an arms merchant."

"I am an arms merchant as well," replied Manoah.

"Yes, Manoah, I know that. It is not the same."

"The matter is settled. Samson will marry this young lady. We will welcome her as our daughter-in-law."

"Manoah, you have long been an esteemed member of our community. Your farm and business have prospered. Some say it is a blessing from God, others say it is a test from God to see how your son the judge will fare. Samson now allying himself with the Philistines can lead to no good. We cannot force you to do anything, but be warned. This will come to a bad end."

Samson, who had been silent during this conversation, spoke. "Master Priest, I have a question for you."

"Yes, what is it?'

"When I was a boy, you yourself trained me. Did you not teach me that God told Abraham that he would be a blessing to all of the nations?'

"Yes, I taught you that. What has that to do with this matter?'

"How can we be a blessing to the nations if we do not mingle, join, and marry with them? How can we do that?"

"The Lord God did not tell Abraham to mix with them. You can bless them without marrying them."

"I think that when we hold ourselves apart from them, they think we are too high-minded. They think that we think we are better than them and scorn us for it."

"We are the people God chose to bring His message to the world, Samson."

"Yes, precisely. And we cannot bring the message if we cut ourselves off from them."

"When we mix with them, we abominate ourselves and start following their idols and false gods."

"Is that their fault or ours? If we change our ways because of them, the fault is ours. Why can we not be faithful to our beliefs and still live with them?"

"It is a fine sentiment to say that we can, but it does not happen. Look at what happened to us in Egypt. We lived among them so long that we became like them. Right away in the desert, when we thought Moses was gone, we built an idol to worship. We wanted to sell our heritage and return to the pottage of Egypt. When things are going well for us, we turn from God and follow our own will."

"Yes, we did then, and we still do. So what is the difference if one faithful man of Israel marries a Philistine woman and teaches her about His God?"

"You will do as you please, Samson. That much is clear. But do not expect our blessing on it."

"I did not and have not asked for it. I have all the blessing I need from my father and mother and from my Father, the Lord God."

"Is He indeed your Father?"

"Is He not yours?"

The priest left the house.

Sixty days later, Samson was ready to return to Timnah. He set out with his parents on the same road as before.

When they approached the vineyards of Timnah, they each turned off the road to skirt around them as they had done before. Samson went deliberately past the place where he had slain the lion. There, he saw a very strange sight. A swarm of bees hovered around the carcass. They had made a hive and were building it up within the frame of the lion's ribs. Samson dismounted his horse and approached the body. He knew that part of his vow was to not touch things that were dead, but the priests who had instructed him as a boy were not clear about this rule or how strict it was.

Samson dipped his hand into the body of the lion. He stood almost perfectly still and let the bees swarm around him. When they did not sting him, he reached deep into the cavity and pulled out his hand covered with honey. He tasted it. It was delicious. Samson had an oilskin pouch at his waist that contained small cakes his mother had baked for their journey. He opened it, reached once more into the lion, and scooped out more honey, which he let it drip onto the oilskin. Then he folded it up and tied it back to his belt. Mounting his horse again, he went down through the hills to the road that went into Timnah.

Just outside of town, Samson caught up with his parents. "Look, Mother. Something sweet for you." He held out the oilskin and showed her the honey.

"Where did you get this, Samson?" she asked.

"I found a hive up in the hills and scooped this out. Try it. It is delicious."

Both Zelponi and Manoah dipped their fingers into the honey and tasted it. They, too, thought it was delicious.

After settling in at the inn where they had stayed during their previous trip, they sent a messenger for Booleon to meet them to make the final arrangements for the marriage. Papers were signed again, and the bride price was paid to Booleon in gold coins. He grinned broadly as he looked at the coins. It was more money than he made in a year of running his business. Had he known that having daughters was so prosperous, he might have married again and had more. He wondered how much he might get for Merari's sister, Netta.

When the day of the wedding arrived, Samson was in high spirits. The ceremony, performed in the back room of the Red Boar Inn, was short. A priest of Dagon, the chief god of the Philistines, came. He killed a small calf and placed the entrails in a bowl beneath the entwined hands of Samson and Merari. He mumbled some words and waved his hands over the bowl. Zelponi recoiled at this, yet she could not help remembering what the priests had done to try to remedy her barrenness, which was eerily similar. When the priest was finished, he declared the couple married and shouted that the feasting could begin.

The Philistines were famous for their feasts. There were more taverns and inns in Timnah than in the entire tribal territory of Dan. Now they brought out skins filled with wine and flagons of other strong spirits. They drank and sang and danced. Musicians played tambourines and drums and flutes. Samson laughed and danced with his bride. He and his mother drank nothing but water, but his father had his share of wine and grew quite merry. Samson's parents refrained from eating anything but bread and fruits. They disdained the meat, as they had no idea what might have been offered to the god Dagon, and they would not defile themselves with meat burned to false gods. Samson did not worry about that and ate the meat freely.

When the evening was drawing to a close, Samson stood up and offered a toast to his new Philistine friends. "I am rejoicing here with you today," he said. "Celebrating the beauty of my new bride. To make the festivities even more exciting, I have a riddle for you. If you can guess the riddle within the seven days of feasting, I will give you thirty fine-linen garments and thirty suits of clothes. I know how you prize the clothes made by my people. Will that not be a fine prize? However, if you cannot solve the riddle, you must give me thirty linen garments and thirty suits of clothes. Will you agree?"

The entire room erupted with "Yes, yes! Tell us the riddle. We agree!"

"Then I will tell it to you," Samson replied. "Here it is. Out of the eater, something to eat. Out of the strong, something sweet. That is my riddle."

"What type of riddle is that?" Commander Phicol shouted from the back of the room.

"It is my riddle. Can you not solve it, Commander Phicol? I assure you there is an answer."

"Then we will solve it!" Phicol replied, and shouts of affirmation echoed around the room.

"Then we will meet here again tomorrow to continue the feast!" Samson shouted.

With that, Samson and his wife retired to the house of Booleon, where they would live until Samson could build a house of their own near the home of his parents.

Merari's room served as the bridal chamber. There, Samson watched as his wife cleaned herself with damp cloths after she had removed her clothes. He marveled at the white smoothness of her body, the gentle curve of her hips, and the sharper curve of her breasts. Samson was gentle with her and slow to act, as he had never had a woman before. Their lovemaking lasted long into the night, and the morning found them exhausted and spent in each other's arms.

On the second night of the feast, the revelry continued. Once again, at the end of the evening, Samson stood and challenged his guests. "Have you no answer to the riddle yet? I am waiting for you."

There was no answer.

"Then my wife and I will retire to await your pleasure tomorrow."

For three nights this continued, and the Philistines had no answer for the riddle. Samson's parents had left to return home after the first night, and now he was alone and enjoying himself at the expense of the Philistines.

PHICOL: THE COMMANDER

On the fourth night of Samson's wedding feast, Commander Phicol went and sat near Merari while Samson was talking to some of the other men in the party. "Do you know the answer to this riddle, my dear?" he asked.

"No, Commander, I do not."

"Then I suggest you get the answer from your husband. Did you invite us here to rob us of suits of clothes?"

"No, Commander. Of course not."

"Then get me the answer. If you do not, it will not go well with you and your family. We will burn your father's house to the ground with all of you in it. Do you understand me?"

"Yes, Commander. I understand."

That night, Merari pleaded with Samson.

"Tell me the answer to the riddle, my love."

"I did not even tell my parents before they left. Why should I tell you? They will not guess it, and when I tell them the answer, you will know it also."

Merari cried and cried that night and refused to come to bed or let Samson console her.

Each night after that, Merari repeated the same scene. She was desperate to save her family. Still, it never occurred to her to tell Samson what Commander Phicol had said and trust Samson to save them. She was too afraid of Phicol and the Philistine army. She was certain they would do as Commander Phicol had said.

Finally, on the morning of the seventh day, Samson relented. "You will worry me to death," he said. "I will tell you." He related the story to her of his killing the lion and finding the honey, thus explaining the riddle. Merari was amazed by this story of Samson's great strength that destroyed a mighty lion.

At the feast that night, Commander Phicol approached her as soon as they came in the door. "How are you tonight, dear bride?" he asked. "It is the last night of the feast. Have you any information for us?"

Samson had gone across the room and was talking to some of the men about making armor and the fine quality of his father's swords. Merari told Phicol the answer to the riddle. She was ashamed of herself but thought, *What else can I do?* She hoped there would not be any trouble because of what she had done. Perhaps Samson would think they had just guessed the riddle.

As the night drew to a close, Samson stood up as he had before. "Well, my friends, this is our last night together. This is your final chance to answer my riddle. What is it to be? Clothes for me or clothes for you?"

Commander Phicol stood up. "I think I might have an answer, Samson."

"Then speak, Commander. What is it?"

"What is sweeter than honey? What is stronger than a lion?'

Samson looked across the room at Merari seated at their table. She would not look at him. His cheeks burned, and his blood churned with anger. "You would not have guessed my riddle if you had not plowed with my heifer, Commander."

"Have I guessed it rightly?"

"Yes, you will get your clothes and garments. Do not worry."

With that, Samson stormed from the tavern. He walked to Booleon's house, mounted his horse, and rode off into the night at a full gallop down the road to the city of Ashkelon. He was furious. His wife had betrayed him. He did not know the reason for her betrayal, nor did he care. He only knew that his wedding had been ruined, and now he wanted revenge on the Philistines. For the first time in his life, he hated them.

Why could they have not been honorable and either guessed the riddle or admitted they could not? Instead, they had cheated. He was sure that Phicol was behind it all. Had he not spied him talking to his wife from across the room? Now he wanted revenge, but he did not know how to get it.

Samson stopped at a small tavern in Ashkelon and asked for water to drink. He placed a gold coin on the table when the waiter brought it.

"The water here is free, my friend," the waiter said. "We only charge for the wine and the other drinks."

"I would rather pay for the water," Samson replied.

"As you please. I will be happy to take your gold."

Samson looked around the room. It was crowded with men drinking and making merriment with songs and ribald jokes. He counted them. There were thirty or more in the room. An evil thought came into Samson's head. *Thirty men here, thirty suits of clothes and linen garments. Why should I pay for the treachery of the Philistines?* He stood up. The door to the tavern had a long wooden plank that went across it to lock it from the inside. Samson strode to the door and placed the wooden plank across the door.

"Hey, what are you doing there?" called the proprietor with a laugh. "How can our customers get in?"

Samson walked back into the room. He felt hot inside, and his brain was racing. Then, without warning, he struck. One after another, the Philistine men fell under the onslaught of his bare fists. One blow for each man was all it took, and they fell, all of them. Some tried to jump on Samson's back and wrest him to the ground, but he shrugged them off like flies and smashed them to the floor.

In a few minutes, it was over. There were several women in the room, but he did not touch them. Slowly, he made his way around the room, stripping the clothes from his victims. The women stood in a corner of the room, terrified of this terrible man who had killed these thirty-plus men with such ease. When Samson was finished, he tied the clothes in a bundle, removed the plank from the door, and walked out of the tavern.

He rode back along the road to Timnah. At the tavern of the Red Boar Inn, some of the men from the wedding feast were still there, drinking. They did not like for a feast to end, even when it was time.

Samson walked in and threw the clothes on the floor in the middle of the room. "These are for Commander Phicol and his friends. I hope he lives as long as the men who wore them before him."

Samson left and once more mounted his horse. He would go back to his father's house to rest and think about this matter more.

When Booleon heard that Samson had left, he signed new papers to give Merari to one of the supposed friends of the groom from the feast. As far as he was concerned, Samson had ended the marriage.

When Samson returned home, it was with a heavy heart. He did not know how to tell his mother and father what had happened. The Philistines had made a fool of him, and now he wanted revenge. He was angry with himself for having revealed the riddle to Merari but was angrier with Phicol. Samson hated him and vowed that he would get back at Phicol, for he was certain it was Phicol who had done it.

Manoah and Zelponi were kind to Samson as he slowly poured out his tale of woe. They did not upbraid him for his foolishness or remind him that he had been warned. They merely welcomed him home and then left him alone to sort things out for himself.

Samson brooded in the house for weeks on end. He took long walks in the fields as the time for harvest approached and watched the grain ripening and the heads blossoming golden in the sun. When two months had passed, he could stand it no longer. He took a young kid goat from his father's herd and announced that he was going back to Timnah.

"I want to see Merari," he said. "Perhaps this offering of a young goat will show that I do not hate her for what she did."

"That is wise of you, my son," Manoah responded. "It is a truly great man of God who can forgive such betrayal. You will show yourself to be better than your enemies."

When Samson reached Timnah, he went straight to the house of Booleon and knocked at the door. Booleon opened the door and stared at him, astounded.

"Samson. Why are you here?'

"I have come to see Merari. I brought this peace offering to her. Tell her that her husband is here."

"Samson, my boy, I cannot. You see, according to the law of the Philistines, you did not complete the marriage week, and so I gave her to one of the groomsmen."

"How could you give away my wife? She is bound to me! We signed a marriage contract!"

"Yes, but the contract required you to complete the week of feasting and sacrifices. It was not completed. Please, do not be angry. Listen to me. Merari has a sister, Netta. She is even more beautiful than Merari and younger as well. Would she not make a better bride for you? I will give her to you and require no further bride price. Please, accept this offer."

"I want the wife who was given to me. I want to talk to her and find out why she betrayed me."

"Samson, she told me everything. They threatened to kill us all. They said they would burn down my house and all of us in it. She was only protecting us. She was afraid they would surely kill us."

"Why did she not tell me this? I could have protected you from them. Did she not know that a man who can tear a lion in two could protect her from a few Philistines?"

"She was afraid, I tell you. She is just a foolish young girl. She does not know anything about the way of the world. They frightened her so badly that she was afraid to tell you and then have them kill us anyway."

"Who was it, Booleon? Which one threatened her?"

"Oh Samson, can we not just let this drop? If you do anything else, it will go badly for all of us."

"Who was it, Booleon? Tell me or I may burn your house down myself. You know what I did to those men in Ashkelon. Surely they have told you about that?"

58

"Yes, they were furious about that also. Commander Phicol said he would not accept any clothes with the blood of the Philistines on it. He had the clothes burned in the fire."

"Phicol likes fire, does he? Is he the one who threatened to burn you up?"

"Samson, please leave this place. Take Netta with you, and go back to the land of Dan. I beg you."

"Tell me who it was, Booleon. Was it Phicol?"

"Yes, yes, it was Phicol, and now I am sure he will kill us all. He has spies everywhere. They are probably watching us right now."

"Phicol! I knew it was him. Now he has given me cause to avenge myself against the Philistines."

"What will you do, Samson?"

"I do not know yet, but they will pay, Booleon. They will pay."

Samson leaped on his horse and rode away from Timnah. He rode up into the hills outside the town and sat down on a rocky promontory overlooking the valley. Beneath him laid the grain fields and vineyards of Timnah. He sat for many hours, looking down on the fields.

Soon night fell. Some foxes crept past him down the path toward the fields. Samson was sitting quietly and he was upwind from them so they did not sense his presence. When he saw them, he jumped up and landed right on top of them, grabbing them by the scruff of their necks. He thrust them into a blanket he had brought with him and tied the ends together. Now a plan began to hatch in his mind. He would use the foxes and fire to enrage the fox Phicol, who loved fire so much!

Samson spent the next several weeks in the hills and fields around Timnah. One by one, he trapped and imprisoned foxes and tied them neck to neck with a stout rope they could not chew through. He then secured this rope around a large boulder in a cave that he had discovered in the hills.

When he had collected three hundred foxes, he slowly tied them together with their tails joined by a shorter piece of rope. In the middle of this rope, he set a torch covered with a cloth soaked in pitch. Then, pair by pair, he lighted the torches and released the foxes into the grain fields, which were fully grown and ripe for harvest, just as the fields of his father had been. Before long, they were all ablaze as the foxes ran in terror through them, seeking in vain to loose themselves. When the torches finally burned down to the ropes, they burned through them, and the foxes ran free. It was an ingenious plan, and it worked perfectly.

Samson would not enter the vineyards himself, but he walked around the outskirts and threw torches there as well. He also set fire to the olive groves. Before long, the entire countryside around Timnah was ablaze. Samson stayed in the hills and watched as the Philistines tried to douse the fires, but he had spread them too well. Now his revenge was complete. He laughed to himself as he watched them scurry around the valley below him.

In the village of Timnah, the people were in an uproar. The farmers were blind with rage and demanded that Commander Phicol find out who had perpetrated this terrible deed. All of their crops for the season had been destroyed, and they would pay dearly for it for years to come.

Phicol, with his usual efficiency, had his spies report to him. One of them stepped forward in a meeting at the Red Boar. "I know who caused all of this, Commander," he said.

"Then tell me, man. Who was it?"

"It was Samson, the son-in-law of Booleon. I saw him at the home of Booleon a few weeks past. I did not know why he was there, but it seems that he came back for his wife. But she has been given up to one of our brethren, and Samson was enraged about it. I could not hear the whole conversation as I stood at the corner of Booleon's house, but I know that your name was mentioned."

"Why did you not report this to me sooner, Bortis?"

"I thought nothing of it, Commander. Samson left, and I thought he had returned to his country. But now I am certain it was he. Who else would do this to us?"

"Yes, who else indeed. Samson, eh? Well, we shall have to teach Booleon a lesson after all. Come with me. We will pay him a visit. Get a hammer and some nails, and bring them along and also several torches."

Phicol led a procession of seven men to Booleon's house. Phicol knocked loudly on the front door, and Booleon soon appeared.

"Hello, Booleon." Phicol practically purred the greeting. "How are you on this fine day?"

"Commander. I am fine, sir. And how are you?"

"I am well, Booleon. But I confess that I am a bit disturbed."

"Disturbed about what, Commander?"

"I have a report that young Samson was here some weeks ago. Is that so?"

"Yes, my lord, Commander. It is so."

"Why did you not report this to me?"

"He threatened to kill me and my family. I was frightened to death for the sake of my daughters."

"And you are not frightened to death of me?"

"You have always been a just man, Commander. You knew what a threat Samson was. I was sure you would know he was here and deal with him yourself."

"Yes, I might have known if my spies had possessed any sense." He looked at Bortis with an evil gaze. "However, like you, they were foolish. Now, my dear friend, you will have to pay for your foolishness."

"I beg you, Commander. Have mercy on us. This man Samson has beguiled us. We were sorely afraid of him when we heard how easily he killed thirty men. What would he have done to us?"

"That is not an important question now, is it?"

Phicol signaled to one of his men, who went to the rear of the house and nailed the back door shut. He then returned to the front.

"Bortis, you will go into Booleon's house with him, and stay there until I call for you. Guard the place well, and allow nobody to leave the house. Do you understand?"

"Yes, Commander. I understand."

Bortis entered the house with Booleon and closed the door behind him. Phicol gave a silent signal, and another soldier nailed the front door shut. Phicol then threw the torches up on the roof made of thatch.

"The rest of you will stay here," he ordered. "Nobody comes out of this house under penalty of your own death. Three of you stand at the rear door and three stand here. Are my instructions clear?"

"But what of Bortis, Commander?" one of the soldiers asked.

"I said nobody comes out!"

"Yes, Commander," they responded with one voice.

By nightfall, the house was burned to the ground. Nobody escaped.

In the early hours of the morning, Samson appeared on the outskirts of the town and saw what was left of Booleon's house. He rode up to the cinders and the black stumps from the wooden frame and dismounted. He stood, waiting, for he knew that soon Phicol would appear.

At midday, one of Phicol's men passed by. Realizing that it was Samson standing and waiting next to the remains of Booleon's house, he rushed to get the commander.

Phicol was hesitant to approach Samson, but he knew that the people of the city were watching him, so he could not back down from this insolent Israelite now. He rode up to Samson and remained in the saddle. A hundred soldiers surrounded Samson, waiting for Phicol to speak.

"Well, Samson, dear son of Manoah. You have returned. It is too bad that your bride's family is not here to greet you, but they have gone to live elsewhere now. We burned their house in memory of the hot time you caused us."

"And I suppose they were in the house when you burned it."

"Samson, you wound me deeply! Do you think we are barbarians who would do such a thing?"

"I put nothing past you, Phicol. I trust you less than the foxes I set free in the fields. They, like you, are true to their nature. You can depend on them to do what they were bred to do. You were bred to destroy, and destroy you will."

"We all have our place in the world, Samson. We just need to know what that place is."

"I know my place, Phicol. Do you know yours? Now you have given me true cause to take revenge against you, and I will not stop until I get it. You are a coward, Phicol, to kill my wife and her family like this. Now I will prove you are a coward in front of all these men of yours. Phicol the coward will run for his life!"

With that, Samson exploded in the middle of the soldiers. In such close quarters, they could hardly touch him for fear of injuring each other. He was like a wild man, thrashing about. He lifted one soldier and used him like a club to knock down the others. Phicol's horse reared up, and Samson stepped forward and hit it a tremendous blow on its side. The horse fell to the ground, and Phicol scrambled off at the last minute. His soldiers rushed in to help him, crowding around Samson. He flailed at them, and they tumbled down around him, falling like flies swatted by a giant hand.

In blind panic, Phicol ran. He leaped on the horse of one of his men and galloped out of the city. Samson continued his mayhem, and the soldiers ran also. Before long Samson was alone, surrounded by dead and injured soldiers. To those still alive, he said, "See? Your commander is not so brave as he would have you think. He has run like the dog that he is. He is a coward, as I said. I could kill all of you now if I wished, but I am going to leave you alive so you can tell the rest of the Philistines what their hero Phicol is really like. Tell Phicol that Samson of Dan will see that this tale of cowardice is told all throughout the land of Canaan. Phicol the commander has run for his life before Samson the eagle of Dan!"

Samson made his way quickly back to his home. Now he feared for the life of his mother and father. He knew that Phicol would look for every possible way to get back at him. When he returned to his father's house, he told Zelponi and Manoah what had happened to Merari. They were saddened and distressed that Phicol had become such a threat to their son.

"You must leave this place now, Father," Samson pleaded. "It will not be safe for you here. The harvests are almost all in, and the forge can be closed for a time. You have no further need of money, and providing more arms to the Philistines would be foolish right now."

"Yes, Son," Manoah replied. "Perhaps it is time to close the forge for good. We have enough money to last several lifetimes. The forge has served its purpose, and the time for it is past. I will pay two year's wages to each of the workers so they will have time to adjust and find other work."

"But you both need to leave here for a time. They will come looking for me. I am sure of that. I will go into the hills near Etam and hide. They will never find me there. You must go to the north, perhaps into the land of Zebulun or Issachar near the Sea of Galilee. It is supposed to be beautiful country there."

"Yes, Son. We will go."

"When things get quiet here again, I will send for you."

Samson helped his father with the affairs of closing the shop and putting their lands into the care of the local governor. Then he hugged his parents and said his farewells. "Good-bye, Father and Mother. May God watch between us while we are apart and bring us safely back together again."

Zelponi cried as she hugged her son. "Be careful, my darling boy. Do not let them catch you."

"Do not worry, Mother. I will be careful."

So it came to pass that Samson went to live in the hills of the land of Judah, which was south of the countryside of Dan and wrapped around the land of the Philistines. When the Philistines rose up, it was often Judah that suffered first, and it was Judah that had given up so much land as the Philistines pushed their borders northward.

For months, Phicol sent raiding parties into the land in search of Samson without success. Finally, he led a force of several thousand men into the land of Judah and camped near Lehi in Judah. The leaders of Judah went out to meet him. At their head was a man named Akim, the oldest of the tribal commanders of Judah. He rode up to Phicol's tent where he was seated in a small chair under the front awning.

Akim remained on his horse as he spoke. "What is it you want with us, and why this show of force?"

Phicol sat drinking from a goblet of wine and smiling. "We have come looking for Samson. We believe you know where he is. We will stay here until we find him or you turn him over to us. If you do not, we will lay waste to this land as he laid waste to our fields and vineyards. Many of us may die, but so will many of you. Why should you all die for the sake of one man? Find Samson, bring him to us, and we will leave peacefully. We will only pay him back for what he did to us."

"Give us time, and we will search for him," Akim replied.

After a great deal of arguing among themselves about what to do, the men of Judah sent out a force of three thousand men to look for Samson. Nobody knew those hills like the men of Judah, and in the course of several days, they found Samson in a cave near the rock called Etam.

Samson came out to meet them. "What is it you want?" he asked.

"What are you doing to us, man of Dan? Don't you know that the Philistines rule over us here? We are their closest neighbor in Israel, and we suffer most when they rise up. What have you done to us by coming here? Why have you so enraged them against you?"

"I only did to them what they did to me. Fire for fire, death for death. You would have done the same if it had been your wife slaughtered."

"We have come here in peace, Samson. We have no fight with you. Your mother is from our tribe, and we honor you and her. But the Philistines want you, and if we do not deliver you to them, we will have war and many will die."

"So what do you intend to do?" Samson asked.

"We will tie you up and hand you over to them, and then they will leave."

"I am willing to go with you and let you tie me. Only swear to me that you will not kill me yourselves to please the Philistines."

"We agree. We will only tie you up and hand you over to them. We will not kill you. Let our word be as the word of God to you."

So the men of Judah tied Samson with two new ropes and led him from among the rocks. When they reached the camp of the Philistines near Lehi, they left Samson with his captors and returned to their homes.

Samson stood bound in front of a force of three thousand men. Phicol came forward, astride his horse, and his men came behind him, shouting and waving their weapons, chanting what Phicol had taught them, "Kill Samson! Kill Samson! Kill Samson of Dan!"

"So, Samson, we meet again," Phicol said.

"Yes, Commander Coward. The last I saw of you, I was looking at the other end of your horse as you ran away. I told your men then that you were a coward, and I repeat it here today." Then he shouted as loud as he could. "Phicol, your commander, is a coward. He proved it before in Timnah. Now watch. All of you watch closely as he proves it again here today."

Then the Spirit of God came upon Samson. He snapped the ropes like they were mere flax. On the side of the roadway, he had seen the carcass of a donkey. He snatched up the jawbone and began flailing it like a sword, slashing one way and then the other. The soldiers rushed in toward him, but he was among them like a demon, smiting to the right and to the left. Their swords and spears were unable to pierce his skin. They dropped dead by scores around him, and then panic seized the rest of them and they ran, eyes wide with fear.

Phicol turned his horse and began riding away from the carnage. What he saw put a new kind of fear into his soul. In Timnah, there had only been one hundred men at his command. Now there were three thousand, and he knew they would all die at the hands of Samson if they did not run.

Samson ran up beside Phicol's horse and, reaching up, slashed at him with the jawbone. He cut the left side of Phicol's face from the forehead to the lower jaw. Phicol rode on in blind fear, blood streaming down from the wound.

"Run, Phicol, run!" Samson shouted. "Run, you coward of a Philistine! Run for your life!"

In the span of a half hour, Samson had finished the destruction. Bodies lay all around him, a thousand or more. There were too many to count. He stood in their midst, exhausted, his arms hanging by his sides now as the strength God had given him subsided. He walked away from the scene exalted and with the flush of excitement that comes only from victory in a great battle. Then he sang a tune:

"With a donkey's jawbone
I made donkeys of them.
With a donkey's jawbone
I killed a thousand men."

The men of Judah, who later discovered the scene, reported that it might well have been two thousand men who were killed. Nobody counted the bodies as they were stripped of their armor. The men of Judah had given up Samson, and now they profited from their betrayal. But Samson did not care. He threw down the jawbone, and the place became known ever after as Jawbone Hill.

As he walked away from the scene, Samson became so thirsty that he thought he would faint from lack of water. He cried out to God, "You have given your servant this great victory. Must I now die of thirst and fall into the hands of the uncircumcised?"

In moments, before Samson's eyes, a hollow opened up in a rock in front of him and out of it flowed fresh, clear water. Samson rushed forward and fell down to drink from the rock. As he drank, his strength revived, and he left that place, never to return. To this day, it is called The Spring That was Called Open.

DELILAH: THE GODDESS

For many years after Samson's near destruction of Phicol's forces, there was peace in the land. The Philistines had been badly demoralized, and Phicol's status as commander was severely impaired. Although he retained his position and had charge over many men, they did not respect him, and he knew it. He curtailed his activity north of Timnah and kept to policing the town and the surrounding area, deciding it best to leave Samson alone.

In the meantime, Samson's stature as a judge had grown tremendously. He was revered as a hero in Judah, and the tales of his exploits spread throughout the land.

Samson had a force of a thousand men at his command that guarded over Zorah, and his spies all around the area kept a close watch for any activity on the part of the Philistines. He built large guard compounds, each holding one hundred men, at ten-mile intervals for one hundred miles in all four directions from the home of his father. They were stationed there year round, guarding the route along every possible road the Philistines could travel. Their sole task was to guard Samson's parents, who had returned to their home, and to watch and report anything suspicious to Samson.

Through the years, Samson had many adventures, though none so repeated like the battle at Lehi. He continued his forays into the Philistine territory, sometimes disguised by shabby clothes that covered his bulk and manly features. Samson was not a fool, but he loved the idea of fooling the Philistines and listening at their inns and taverns as they told the tale of Samson. He went also in the guise of a cloth merchant, taking bolts of cloth his mother had purchased for him and selling them in the bazaars and markets of Timnah, Ashkelon, and Gaza. At these times, he walked with a shambling gait or hunched himself over, or covered one of his eyes with a cloth as though he were blind in that eye. He also disguised himself with false hair and beards. He bargained with the merchants like a seasoned vendor, and they did not know they were bargaining with their old enemy, Samson.

"This sash is beautiful, is it not?" he asked one vendor in the market. "It is said it was once worn by the strong man Samson. Perhaps it has his power sewn into it. Who can know?"

"Do You take me for an idiot?" the vendor asked. "Everyone knows that his strength comes from his weapons. His father is a mighty weapons maker, and the weapons are filled with magic and the power of his god."

"Oh no, Master. I had not heard that tale. It was the weapons that did it, you say? Perhaps I could get some of them. Would you be interested in purchasing the sword of Samson?"

"You are a crippled old fool. Nobody can get his weapons. They are kept in his fortress stronghold in the north. Nobody knows where it is except among the high crags of the land north of us."

"Ah Master, you are very wise to know such things."

So Samson's life continued.

One day, Samson went down to Gaza to spy, pretending to sell cloth and dishes, and met a prostitute there named Tirzah. He spent the night with her and revealed who he was. At first, she did not believe him, but when he took off his clothes, she saw that he was no ordinary street vendor.

Late in the evening, she told him she was going out to get them food for their supper. She quickly called some of the Philistine soldiers she knew and told them who was in her house. They did not believe her, but when she described Samson, they decided they had better see for themselves. They told her to wait until Samson was asleep and then early in the morning leave the house. They would come there to get him. They quickly dispatched runners to all of the nearby encampments, calling for assistance, as they were afraid to attack the strong man of Israel without an army behind them.

Samson suspected Tirzah when she returned. She acted nervous and afraid. They ate their meal and enjoyed love early in the night and then fell asleep.

Samson quietly got up before half the night was gone. He walked out toward the city gates, and there he saw a company of soldiers, lying in wait for him. He rushed forward and pulled at the gates, one by one. He tore them loose and pulled up the massive posts that supported them as well. Awakened, the soldiers ran in fear. They knew what Samson had done to thousands of their fellows, and they dared not lift a hand against him.

Samson hefted the gates to his shoulders and carried them away from the city. He took them to the top of a hill that faces the city of Hebron, miles away from Gaza, and left them there. He laughed when thinking of the soldiers, representing the might of Philistia, cowering and running from the gates they were supposed to guard. He thought perhaps they might not look to ambush him there again.

As Samson grew older, his thoughts turned to having a family. He missed the companionship that can only come from a wife and children. He wondered what his life might have been had he been a normal man, living out his days as a blacksmith or a farmer. He knew his parents were getting older and wished he could give them grandchildren. When such thoughts came to his mind, he grew melancholy and lonely.

One day, Samson went down into the valley of Sorek, south of his home in Zorah. There were numerous small villages there, but he had seldom visited them in his travels. In one such village, he stopped at a wayside inn for the night. In the dining room was a girl waiting tables. When Samson looked at her, a longing in his chest caused his breath to shorten and his eyes to ache. The girl was beautiful, but that was not what caused this feeling in him. He had seen many beautiful girls before. Merari had been beautiful, but she had never made him feel like this.

It dawned on Samson that he loved the girl and was feeling the pangs of love he had heard other men describe. He had never felt them before. Perhaps he had never loved Merari. That thought troubled him, but he did not dwell on it. Merari was dead, and no matter what, she had been his wife. He could not think of her without it causing him pain. No, Samson knew that this girl was different. She moved differently than other women, almost gliding across the floor with her tray of food and drinks. Her long, raven-colored hair fell almost to her waist.

Samson was afraid to speak to her. The strong man of Israel, afraid for the first time in his life, and of a woman! Finally, he plucked up his courage and spoke to her.

"Here, lovely one. Stop for a moment, and talk to me."

"I am working, my lord," she answered.

"That is quite alright. Your master has seen my gold. He will not mind your speaking to me for a moment."

The girl looked over to the proprietor of the inn with a question in her eyes. He had overheard their brief conversation and nodded. She sat down at the table across from Samson.

"I can sit for a little while," she said.

"That is good. What is your name?"

"I am called Delilah."

"Delilah. That is a beautiful name. What does it mean?"

"I am not sure. The people of Israel have told me that it means night."

"Night? That is interesting. Where do you come from?"

"My parents were born in Egypt. They came here when I was a little baby. They both died from the plague, and a Hebrew family here raised me. They gave me the name Delilah because my parents came in the middle of the night and asked them to care for me."

"Are you like the night, dark and mysterious?"

"I do not think so. I love the daytime and wandering among the hills. It is lovely here, especially in the spring when everything is in bloom."

"Yes it is lovely here."

"What is your name?"

"I am Samson. My name is the opposite of yours, as it represents the sun that shines in the daytime."

"Are you the Samson they all talk about? The mighty man of Israel who destroyed the entire Philistine army?"

"I am the only Samson. I did not destroy their whole army, but I certainly dealt it a severe blow. Of course, it would be better to say that my God dealt it a severe blow by my hand."

"I often hear our customers talk about you. You are not so big as I imagined."

"I am sorry to disappoint you."

"You did not disappoint me. I just had a vision of your being a giant like a mighty oak tree as tall as the sky."

"I am not quite that tall, but I am a bit taller than most of my brethren."

"You are tall enough. I did not mean to offend you. It is just that when you hear tales about great warriors, you get a picture of them in your mind. I pictured you as a giant!"

"I am no giant, just a man of Israel. Do you have no husband, Delilah?"

"No, I have never been married, though some have asked. I have not found a man to suit me."

"And what kind of man do you think would suit you?"

"I do not know. I suppose a mighty man, a man who would take care of me and keep me safe."

"I would certainly keep you safe if you were mine."

"Are you proposing to marry me?"

"No. I was married once already. It was not a good experience. I have to be careful. The Philistines are always looking for ways to trap me. And what better way than with a wife? They did it to me once already. That is enough."

"That is very sad for you, to have to be so afraid of them that you cannot even take a wife."

"I am not afraid of them. I just have to be careful. Where do you live?"

"I live here at the inn. I have a room upstairs."

"Can I come and stay with you for a while?"

"That is up to Eldon, the innkeeper. He pays my wages. It is up to him to decide."

"Why? Are you a prostitute that you work for him?"

"No, I am not. My foster parents were killed by a raiding band of Philistines. I was working here then, and Eldon offered to let me live here. He and his wife have been like a third set of parents to me. They pay my keep, give me a place to live, and provide me with work to pay my expenses. I owe a lot to them and would not do anything without their approval."

"Do not worry then. I will speak to him and make sure he approves."

Samson moved into the inn and began living with Delilah. He grew to love her more each day. He took her for long walks among the hills surrounding the valley. They talked of many things, but he hesitated to tell her too much about himself or his family. He had a hard time bringing himself to trust her, as he had been betrayed twice by women already. He did not want it to happen again. He also thought that the less she knew, the better for her. If the Philistines ever questioned her, she would not have much to tell them.

In the course of time, Delilah grew fond of Samson also. She invited him into her bed, although there was no further talk of marriage between them. Delilah was a virgin, and Samson treated her gently. Although he was advancing in years, his virility was undiminished.

Delilah, for the first time in her life, felt secure. Samson gave her a sense of safety she had never felt before. In his arms, she felt that nothing could hurt her.

As their love grew, Samson went less and less into the more southern parts of the territory of the Philistines. He felt at last that he had found a place for himself and a woman who would keep watch over him as his years advanced and perhaps someday even bring him children. He was happier than he had ever been. He did not take Delilah to meet his mother and father yet, as he still wanted to keep that part of his life as secret as possible. Although the Philistines had not troubled him for years, he knew they were always just over the border, waiting and ready, so he kept up his guard.

One day, Samson was away from the inn, visiting his father and mother. The years of peace with the Philistines had made him more confident of their safety.

A man came into the inn and sat down to have a drink. Delilah approached him. She was alone in the inn, as Eldon had left to buy provisions in a nearby town. "Can I help you, my lord?' she asked.

"Yes, a flagon of your best wine, if you please."

"Yes, my lord, right away."

She returned shortly with the wine and a goblet. "Would the master care for something to eat?'

"No, I am just here for a few moments. Do you live here?"

"Yes, my lord, I do. In a room on the second floor."

"Ah, I see. And you have been here a long time?"

"For many years, Master. Is there anything else I can get for you?"

"Just some information."

"What kind of information?" Delilah drew back from the table. The man's voice had a sudden menace to it that she did not like.

"I am looking for a man. A particular man."

"What man, my lord?'

"A man you would know in a moment if you saw him. His name is Samson."

Delilah could not refrain from gasping at the sound of the name.

"Ah, then you do know him," the stranger said.

Delilah was silent.

"Come, come, my girl. You have not lost your tongue. Do you know this Samson or not?"

"Yes, my lord, I know a man of that name."

"What other man has ever had that name? Then surely you know the man I am looking for."

"I know a man named Samson," Delilah repeated, but her voice was barely audible. Fear gripped her. She was suddenly aware of a bright white scar that ran down the left side of the man's face just next to his eye. It was an ugly, jagged scar that had turned dark along the edges from infection.

The man gave a menacing smile. "Ah, you see my scar, do you? Is it not striking? Who do you think gave it to me? Yes, my lovely, it was Samson. Samson the bully. Samson the strong man. Samson the hero. Yes, the same Samson you know and are harboring in this inn. The same Samson I mean to destroy if it kills me. Do you hear me?"

"Yes, Master, I hear you." Delilah's voice was barely a whisper.

"Good. Then I have a task for you. A task that will pay you well. Are you a rich woman?"

"No, my lord, I am not. I have nothing."

"That is good because I am going to give you all the wealth your heart could ever desire. All you have to do is find out Samson's secret, the secret of his great strength. I represent all the governors of the Philistines. If you succeed, we will each give you eleven hundred shekels of silver. Do you know how much money that is?"

"No, my lord."

"It is a huge amount. Enough to buy an inn like this many times over. With that much money you will never have to wait on tables again for the rest of your life. Nobody else is ever likely to offer you that much money."

Samson had not told Delilah of the wealth of his family, so she did not know that eleven hundred shekels of silver would be nothing to him. He had a hundred times that much in silver and another hundred times in gold, but he had never spoken to her about that part of his life.

The image of the silver burned in her mind. She felt secure with Samson, but the lure of the silver was a terrible thing. How else could a woman with nothing get such money and the security it would bring? Inside her a battle raged over her devotion to Samson, which had grown considerably, and her lust for the money. And she was afraid of this man with the scar. What could he do to her if she did not help him? Delilah had heard many stories of Samson's great strength, but she had never seen it. Suppose it was just a legend as many were saying, and that those things had never happened as they said they did? She did not know what to do.

"I am afraid to help you, my lord."

"Why? Because of Samson? Yes, I can understand why, but you need have no fear. I am asking you to find out the secret of his strength. We need to know how he can be tied up and subdued. When you find that out, and we take his strength from him, he will not be able to harm you. Until then, we say nothing, and he will have no idea that I have even been here.

"I have many spies in this area. They will start to pass this inn often. Every few nights, starting in one week, one of them will come and will sit at that table back in the corner each time. If the table is taken, he will ask the person sitting there to move. He will order the best house wine, just as I did today. When he does, he will answer your question about something to eat just as I did, saying that he is only here for a moment. If you have found Samson's secret, you will tell him that you will bring him a morsel to eat anyway, as he appears hungry. If you have not found it, you will just bring him the wine. Do you understand?"

"Yes, Master. What will happen then?"

"When you have found his secret and the message is passed to my man, you will walk down into the valley the next day. Tell Samson you just want to get some fresh air by yourself. At the midday hour, I will meet you at the base of the hill opposite this inn. There is a quiet stream there, hidden by a grove of trees. Do you know where it is?"

"Yes, my lord. Samson has walked there with me before."

"Good. Then I will meet you there. By the way, I am a patient man, but there is a limit to my patience. Do not let me wait too long. If I come again to this room, it will be to do mischief you will not like. I hope you understand me. Here, hide this away, and do not by any means let him see it. It is a small down payment."

Commander Phicol threw a rough leather purse onto the table. It was filled with gold coins.

Later, Delilah sat in her room and cried. She did not know what to do. This man Phicol had scared her terribly. In all of her nightmares from childhood, she had never imagined an evil force like him. He was like an ice-cold devil, ready to pounce on her and tear her limb from limb without a single thought.

She had indeed grown to love Samson. Perhaps not with the love he felt for her, but it was genuine and from her heart. Now that love was threatened by the combating emotions of fear and greed. Or perhaps it was not greed at all. Was it greedy to want security and comfort? She knew Samson was not a poor man, as he too carried a hefty purse and wore clothes that would pay her wages for some years. But he had told her nothing of his family or his wealth. She did not know what the weight of his purse meant to her. Suppose he did marry her and then die? What would she have as a woman under the laws of his people? She did not know, and he had given her no occasion to ask since he had not proposed marriage. What could she do?

That night when Samson returned, Delilah tried acting as though nothing had happened, but he saw that she was uneasy.

"What is it, my love?" he asked. "What is bothering you?"

"It is nothing. I was just so lonely today without you here and being by myself. I did not like it."

"I am sorry for that. I had to see my mother and father, as I have not seen them in some time. My father is getting quite old now. I do not know how many years he will still be here, so I have to see him whenever I can."

"You love your mother and father very much, don't you?"

"Yes, I do, and they love me very much. I could not have asked for two better parents. They have always treated me like a king. Without them, I do not know what my life might have been like."

"You are very fortunate to have had parents like that. I wish I could have known my parents. I am sure they would have loved me that way."

"I am sure they would have also."

"Is that the source of your strength, Samson? The love of your parents? It seems to be something you hang onto dearly."

"Yes, I do. I suppose it is a part of my strength. They have always strengthened me in many ways."

"So that is what makes you strong?"

"Why are you suddenly so interested in what makes me strong?"

"I don't know. I guess I just admire you so much. I would like to be more like you, even though I am a woman. If I knew what made you so strong, perhaps I could be strong like that also and would not need to be afraid of anyone."

"With me here you don't need to be afraid of anyone. I will take care of you."

"And if you leave? Who will take care of me then?"

"What has gotten into you, Delilah? Suddenly you act as though the world will end tomorrow. I am not going anywhere. I promise you."

"I hope not, Samson. I hope not."

When they went to bed, Delilah slept uneasily. She awoke several times, drenched with sweat. She dreamt of Phicol and his evil scar. He leered at her in the dream with his eyes popping and a vicious snarl on his lips.

In the morning, she awoke, exhausted from the night. With the coming of the dawn and Samson beside her, she finally felt her fear drifting away. However, each night it was the same, and only the rays of the morning sun streaming through her window gave her comfort.

One week later, a man appeared at the inn just as dusk was approaching. He sat at a table in the far corner of the room. He wore a dark cloak and had a hood over his head, masking his features.

Delilah approached him. "Would you care for a drink, sir?"

"Yes," he replied. "Bring me the best wine in the house."

"Would you care for something to eat also?"

"No, I am just passing by for a moment. Just bring the wine."

"Yes, sir."

Delilah brought the wine and took his coin in payment. He drank the wine quickly and then hurried from the room. After that, another man came every few nights. The same man never came back twice. Each night was a different man, and they were dressed in all manner of clothes. Some were large men who came in laughing and boisterous, drinking down their wine in one large quaff. Others were small and quiet and sipped their wine slowly. But steadily they came, sometimes two nights apart, sometimes three or four, but they always came.

Samson took no heed to this, as travelers along the road past the inn were regular and few nights passed without at least several customers. In any case, he was not always in the room when they came. He often went out to walk when Delilah was tending to her duties at the inn.

When Samson had first come, he had asked Delilah to quit working and let him pay her wages, but she had refused. She did not want to depend on him for her support, she said. Now she wished she had never said any such thing. If she had taken his offer, she might never have met Phicol and had to face his evil stare. But she did not feel she could go back and ask Samson now, as he might get suspicious.

When two weeks had passed, she once again brought up the topic of his strength. "Samson, you have still never told me how you get your strength. Will you not tell me?"

"Are we back to that again? I do not understand this obsession you have with my strength. What difference does it make?"

"Tell me how you can be tied up and subdued. Perhaps I want to tie you up and have my way with you."

"You don't have to tie me up to do that," Samson laughed.

"No, but if you love me as you say, would you not tell me?"

"I have never told anyone, not even the woman who was my wife."

"Will you not tell me, Samson?"

"All right, I will tell you. If you tie me up with seven fresh thongs of leather that have never been dried, I will become as weak as other men."

"Is that really the secret?"

"Yes, it is."

The next night, Phicol's spy came and sat in the corner of the room. Delilah approached him and said, "Can I get you some drink, my lord?"

"Yes," he replied. "Bring me the best wine in the house."

"And to eat, my lord? Nothing to eat?"

"No, I am just passing by quickly. Nothing to eat."

"But, my lord, you look famished. I will bring you a small morsel anyway."

Delilah brought the wine, a small cake and a plate of dates. He ate and drank and then quickly left.

The next day, Delilah told Samson she was going for a walk. He offered to go with her, but she told him no, that she just needed to get away from the inn for a few minutes. At the stream, she met Phicol and told him what Samson had said.

"Do you believe him?" he asked.

"I do not know why he would lie to me."

"I do. We will see. Tonight one of my men will come again. In his cloak he will carry seven fresh thongs of leather. When Samson falls asleep, you will tie him with them. Most of us will be waiting below your window. I will send two men up to the room with you. They will hide behind the curtains that cover the windows. After you have tied him, yell out, 'Samson, the Philistines are upon you! Get up!' Then we will see what happens. If he cannot get up or get loose from the thongs, my men will signal us from the window, and we will come up. If he breaks free, they will give no signal. In that case, you will meet me here again tomorrow. Is that clear?"

"Yes, my lord. How will your men get into the room?"

"There is a room that adjoins yours. One of my men has paid well to secure it for a season. The innkeeper was happy to have us pay many times what he would normally get for it. If Samson breaks the thongs, they will wait until he is asleep again and make their way into the other room. If they have to wait until morning, just make sure you are the one to open the curtains and open them only part way so they can remain concealed."

That night, Delilah was filled with fear and desperation. What would Samson do if he discovered her treachery? Would he kill her? She almost wanted to tell him and let him do so. Could that be worse than facing the evil man who had come to capture him? She did not even know his name, as he had not mentioned it. Nor did she know his connection to the Philistine army. She only knew that he was evil, and that he would stop at nothing to get what he wanted.

When Samson came to bed, he too was restless. She wondered if he suspected anything. If only he would drink wine. Then she could lull him to sleep, and he might not suspect her. But she knew there was no chance for that, as Samson had not touched a drop of wine since she had met him. Could that be the secret of his strength? Perhaps it was.

When Samson finally fell asleep, she waited until she heard him breathing deeply. Then she stole from the bed and got the leather thongs she had hidden among her clothes. Slowly, she tied the thongs over the top of him, fastening them to the posts of the bed, as she could not turn him over for fear of waking him. When she was finished, she waited awhile longer, almost paralyzed with fear of what would happen.

Finally, she cried out, "Samson, Samson, wake up! The Philistines are upon you!"

Samson leaped from the bed, and the thongs snapped like string when it is held next to a flame. Delilah watched in horror, as for the first time she saw the strength of this giant of Israel on display. She had felt the thongs herself and knew that no normal man could break them so easily.

Samson shook himself fully awake and then looked at her curiously. "What game are you playing, Delilah? Where did you get these leather strips?"

"I found them in the cellar. Even Eldon did not know they were there."

"What were you trying to do?"

"You lied to me, Samson. You said those thongs would make you weak, and now you are making a fool of me."

"Oh Delilah, don't be ridiculous. This is just a silly game you are playing."

"It is not a game. Why did you lie?"

"I lied because I didn't know if I could trust you or not."

"Do you trust me now? See? Nothing has happened to you. Will you not tell me the truth now?"

"Yes, Delilah, yes. If you tie me securely with new ropes that have never been used, I will become as weak as other men."

"You are not lying again, are you?"

"No, my love. It is the truth." Samson yawned.

Two days later, one of Phicol's men again came to the inn and was given the same signal. The next day, Delilah went to the stream again to meet Phicol.

"I suppose your lover does not really love you, my girl. He will not share his secret with you."

"Yes, he will. He's told me the truth now. Have your men bring seven ropes that have never been used. You cannot risk giving them to me in the inn again, so take them to the room next to ours and leave them there. Leave the door unbolted, and I will get them later."

"I suppose we will see. The plan will be the same again tonight."

That night, Delilah was no longer afraid, as she was angry with Samson for lying to her. Now she really wanted him to prove his love. Again she waited till he was asleep and then tied the ropes over him. Once more she yelled, "Samson, wake up! The Philistines are upon you!"

Again Samson jumped up and snapped off the ropes like they were strands of thread. Now Samson roared with laughter. "So you are still playing this game with me."

Delilah hit him with her fists in anger. "You are a brute and again have made a fool of me. You say you love me, and then you treat me like this. Why, Samson, why?"

"Oh Delilah, if only you knew what you were asking of me. Come now. Come back to bed."

"No, I will not until you tell me your secret. I mean it this time."

"Yes, Delilah, I will tell you. I have watched you weaving on that loom in the corner of the room. If you weave the seven braids of my hair into the fabric on your loom and tighten it with a pin, I will be as weak as any other man. Now will you come back to bed?"

"Yes, I will."

Delilah decided not to wait another night this time. Samson had not slept well these past nights and was sleeping deeply now. Delilah moved her loom over to the bed and slowly wove the long locks of Samson's hair into a piece of cloth she had been working on. Then she tied the ends of the locks and fastened them with a pin into the frame of the loom. Then she stood up from the bed and yelled, "Samson, wake up! The Philistines are upon you once again!"

The result was the same as before. Samson jumped up and pulled his hair loose, breaking the loom to pieces in the process.

"You see," Delilah said. "You have done it to me again. How can you say you love me and yet won't confide in me? You have lied to me these three times and made me feel like a fool. Go ahead, and go to sleep. Perhaps you should sleep somewhere else, since you do not love me at all."

From that day on, Delilah nagged Samson about his secret. She no longer cared about Phicol and his men.

Finally, it was too much for Samson. One morning, he woke up and found her arranging her hair in front of a bronze mirror. He pulled her into the bed with him.

"You have bothered me to death about my strength. I have had enough. If that is the only way to prove that I love you, I will prove it. No razor has ever been on my head, as I am a Nazirite, set apart to my God by a vow made from the day of my birth. If my head were shaved, I would become as weak as any other man."

"You are telling me the truth this time. I can tell."

"Yes, Delilah, I am telling you the truth."

"Why did you not tell me before?"

"What I have told you I have never told anyone. The priests of Israel know about my vow, but even they do not know what strength can come from being faithful to God and to a vow you have made to Him. The Philistines know nothing about it because they despise our God and think all of our ceremonies and practices are foolish. That is why they have never known the secret of my strength."

"So what is this vow that you took about? Only cutting your hair?"

"No. I cannot drink wine or other fermented drink, and I am forbidden from touching dead things."

"And if your hair was cut, you would become weak?"

"Yes."

"How do you know that, since you have never cut your hair? Suppose you cut it and were still strong?"

"It is the vow that matters, Delilah. I made a vow to God, and as a result, He gave me strength and has protected me all these years. If I break my vow, how can He protect me?"

"I do not know, Samson. I do not know this God. You have mentioned Him from time to time, but I do not know Him. I learned about the gods of the Egyptians when I was a child, and I have heard also of the gods of the Philistines, but I cannot say that I know any of them. Perhaps they are all myths and legends and are not gods at all."

"My God is no myth. What myth could give a man the strength to kill a thousand men?"

"Is that the measure of God then? How many men He can help you to kill?"

"If you understood the Philistines a little better, perhaps you wouldn't say that. They despise all gods but theirs and want to kill anyone who does not recognize their gods. That is why they want to kill me."

"How do you know they want to kill you? Maybe they just want you to stop killing them?"

"Perhaps someday you will understand, Delilah. Now I have told you, so you can stop your tricks and tests and we can live in peace. I worship no God but the one true God, Delilah, but you have become like a goddess to me. I confess that I worship you. If that is a sin before my God, may He have mercy on me."

"Yes, Samson. Yes, my love."

That night, as so often before, the spy came to the inn and, once more, Delilah arranged to meet Phicol by the stream. The next day he was there, waiting for her at the appointed time.

"So what have you found out? The same old tricks?"

"No, this time he has told me everything. I can make him as weak as any man."

"How?"

"By getting him to drink wine. He has made a vow, and if he breaks it by drinking or even having wine touch him, he will become weak."

"By just drinking or touching wine you say? That seems odd and yet I remember when I first met him, something being said about wine disagreeing with his stomach and he did not drink it."

"Yes. Tonight I will prove it to you. I will get him to drink some wine. When he is asleep, I will sing a little song to him. When your men hear the song, have them come out. To prove how weak he will be, I will have them cut off the braids of his hair while he sleeps. Then you can come up. What will you do with him?"

"We will just make sure he can no longer harm us. I have no plans to kill him if he is not a threat."

"Then we will see tonight. What about the silver shekels?"

"I will bring them tonight."

"See that you do."

That night, Delilah bathed and put on her best perfume, the one Samson liked with the scent of attar of roses. She waited for him in bed and then made love to him. As he loved her, she caressed his hair. "Now you have proved that you love me, Samson, by telling me what was in your heart. I love you also. You must know that."

"Yes, my darling. I know that."

Afterward, Samson fell asleep, slouched down on the bed with his head in her lap. She stroked his head and began to sing a soft song that Samson's mother had sung to him when he was a boy. He had taught it to Delilah. "My little boy, my little boy, Samson is my little boy. Rest your head softly now, my little boy."

In a few moments, one of the Philistines came out from behind the curtains over the window. Beside the bed was a small table. Delilah pointed to it, and the Philistine saw a short razor there with a handle of gold. She motioned to the man to pick it up. Slowly and quietly, he came near the bed, and one by one, he gently cut off the seven braids of Samson's hair while Delilah continued stoking his head and humming softly. When the Philistine was finished, he laid the razor back on the table and slowly backed away from the bed. Delilah motioned to him again, and he went to the window. Leaning out, he signaled to Phicol and the other men standing below.

In a few minutes, although they tried to keep quiet, Delilah could hear them coming up the stairs. She kept humming and stroking Samson's head. Then, one by one, the Philistines crowded into the room. There were thirty or more of them. Phicol stood in the front, with a short whip in his hands. When he signaled to Delilah, she rose up and cried, "Samson, get up! The Philistines are upon you!"

As he had done before, Samson leaped up, but he did not know that the Spirit of God had left him. Phicol's men grabbed him, and struggle as he might, Samson could not break free. Phicol struck him several times across the face with the whip.

"So, you dog of a Hebrew, I have you at last. Tie him up quickly!"

They tied Samson with ropes and made him sit on the edge of the bed.

"Now then, Samson," Phicol said. "We have a few scores to settle, I think. First, I have some business to attend to that might interest you."

He turned to Delilah, who was standing by the doorway, shivering.

"Come here, my dear." Phicol spoke to her in what he thought was a soothing voice. "You have no need to fear him any longer. He cannot hurt you now. Come, come. Come over here."

Delilah slowly walked to the bed. Phicol put his arm around her shoulders.

"This is my partner, Samson. The best spy and traitor I have hired in a long time. What all the forces of the Philistines could not do, she has done. Her name will go down in history as the great liberator of the Philistines, right after my name, of course."

Phicol motioned to one of his men who brought two long sacks over to the bed.

"And this is her payment, Samson. Thirteen of the rulers of Philistia provided eleven hundred shekels each. It is all here for her."

Phicol took one of the sacks and placed the leather thong that held it closed, like a necklace around Delilah's neck. It was so heavy that she could not hold it up.

"Look at that, Samson. She has become weak also. She cannot even hoist her reward with the muscles of that delicate neck."

Phicol lifted the sack from around Delilah's neck and threw it onto the bed.

"There you are. Is that better? I know it was a heavy load to carry along with your guilt. The woman who brought down Samson. I still cannot believe it. Now stand him up!"

The men pulled Samson to his feet. Phicol shoved his face into Samson's.

"See the scar you gave me? Look how black it is getting as I get older. There was disease in that donkey, and it got into my skin. Now I will spend the rest of my life remembering you whenever I see myself reflected in the shields of my men. They remember also the humiliation of that day. Now we will give them another day to remember. You almost took one of my eyes that day. Now we will see how you like it."

From under his cloak, Phicol pulled a spoon.

"Hold his head tightly!" he shouted. He grabbed Samson's head and held it under the crook of his arm. With a single, quick motion, he stuck the spoon in Samson's right eye and gouged out the eyeball. It fell out of the socket, still attached to the muscles and ligaments that surround the eyes.

Phicol stepped back and put down the spoon on the table next to the bed. The razor that had been used to cut Samson's hair was still there. Phicol picked it up and, grabbing the eyeball, cut away the tissue until the eye dropped to the floor. Then he grabbed Samson's head again and forced him to look down.

"Look, Samson, for the last time at your right eye."

Samson looked down with his left eye and saw Phicol's foot smash the eye on the floor. Still, Samson did not cry out. Phicol grabbed him again and repeated the gruesome performance with the left eye. Delilah screamed and ran out of the room.

"I guess she has a delicate stomach when it comes to eyeballs on the floor," Phicol laughed. "I can't say I blame her. Now, Samson, we will leave you here tonight. Get some rest, as you have a long journey before you. We are taking you down to Gaza. You remember Gaza, don't you? Yes, of course, you do. There is a millhouse there. We use it as a workplace for special prisoners. You are going to grind for us. You gave us weapons before, and now you will give us bread. Isn't that grand?"

Samson did not speak. The blood ran from his burning eye sockets and soaked the front of his clothes. Pain shot all through his head. Phicol reached out and touched the stream of blood.

"Do not worry about this bleeding, Samson," he said. "I have a physician here with me. He will stop the bleeding for you. I don't want you to die on me before I have a chance to parade you down to Gaza."

The physician came up in a short while. He held some cloths hard against the eye sockets for some time until the bleeding stopped, and then he bathed the area around them in a solution of salt and vinegar, which made the burning worse. When he was finished, he put a salve over the eyelids and wrapped a cloth around Samson's head. Then Phicol spoke once more.

"Now, Samson, we have come to the end of your grand career and the beginning of mine. Tomorrow you will leave this land, so close to where you were born, and you will never return. Do you hear me?"

Samson made no reply.

"Well, it is no matter if you speak or not. I don't blame you. A woman like Delilah would leave me speechless also. She has run off for now, but I am sure she will come back eventually. All that silver, you know. We will not rob her. It will be right here when she gets back, and for us it was a bargain. Now good night, my fine fellow. We will see each other a lot from now on. Oh, pardon me. I guess I will do all of the seeing, won't I? Ha ha ha!"

ZETHAM: THE PRIEST

The morning after his capture, the Philistines pulled Samson up from the bed where he had lain tied all night. They had not bothered to allow him to relieve himself in the night, so his clothes were soiled and wet from his own feces and urine.

"You stink, Samson," Phicol said as he came into the room. "Didn't they even take you to unload yourself? What a shame. Take him down, and wash him off. The cart is here and ready for him."

The soldiers dragged Samson downstairs and threw a bucket of water over him. "We can clean him up better later," one of them said. "Let's get him into the cart."

Samson was pushed roughly onto a large cart with wooden rails around the back. The ropes binding him were tied to the rails with enough slack to allow him to lie down in the cart. Then they started down the road through the valley and out onto the plain below to the road by the sea that led to Gaza. This was an ancient highway, used for centuries by traders from Egypt and Africa. Samson had traveled this road many times on his trips into the land of the Philistines and had always enjoyed it, as it passed so close to the sea. Now as the cart bounced and lurched down the road, he could smell the sea in the distance, knowing he would never set eyes on it again. *I have no eyes!* That thought cycled through his mind in a constant repetition, *I have no eyes!*

The party, made up of several hundred soldiers now, made their way slowly to the south, stopping at several inns and taverns along the way. As always, the Philistines loved their drink. At each of the stops, Phicol came to the back of the cart and splashed some wine on Samson.

"Here you are, Samson. Your ration of wine for the day. Isn't it sweet?"

Samson had no idea why Phicol did this. But it did not bother him. Now that he had opened his heart to Delilah and his vow was broken, nothing else mattered.

"Won't you speak to me any longer, Samson?" Phicol continued. "After all, I didn't cut out your tongue, although I could easily do so. Of course, there is no sense to leave it in if you don't intend to use it. Oh, I suppose you are angry with me. But I don't see why. I didn't betray you. You got from me what you expected, didn't you? You would have done the same to me if you had been in my position. Perhaps you got better, as I am sure you would have killed me."

Samson could not argue with this. He knew it was true. Was it not kinder to just kill your enemy than keep him alive to torture? Still, he was silent.

At last, they reached Gaza. Near the road that continued south from Gaza along the coastline was a large millhouse. Here they drove the cart, and Samson was taken out of the back. They untied the ropes binding him and then stripped off his filthy loin cloth and the bandage from his head. Then they placed bronze shackles on his hands and feet, each connected by a short chain.

It began to rain. Some of the soldiers got wooden poles from the back of the cart and attached them to an oiled cloth which they held over Phicol to keep him dry. Samson stood bound and naked before them, the rain pouring down from the top of his bowed head.

A servant came running from the house when Phicol yelled, "Wodja, come here!" The young man was short and had a child-like appearance that belied his age.

"Yes, Master Phicol," he answered.

"Wodja, this is your new responsibility. Meet Samson, the judge of the Israelites. Samson the mighty, Samson the bold and brave, Samson the hero, brought low by Phicol the Magnificent! He is quite a sight, isn't he, Wodja?"

"Yes, Master."

"He has no eyes, Wodja. We left them behind in his homeland. You will be his eyes now. His life for your life, Wodja. If he should escape, you die. If he should get sick, you die. If he should stub his toe and become useless to us, you die. Do I make myself clear, Wodja?"

"Yes, Master. I die."

"That is a good lad. Just remember that one thing. You die."

"Samson, there is a young man here. He cannot hurt you and will make sure you are treated well. I want you healthy when I bring visitors to see you. Your strength is gone, but you are still a man. You could hurt Wodja if you wished. He will have to come close to you when he feeds you, leads you out to work, and tends to all your other needs. Hurt him at your own peril. I know you do not fear me. Perhaps you think I cannot hurt you anymore, but you are wrong. I have not seen your father in many years. I might not even recognize him if he is still alive, and I only met your mother the one time at your wedding. However, if need be, I can find them. I can find them and bring them here and kill them in front of you. You will not see it, but you will hear it, Samson, that I promise you. I am sure I need to say no more. Take him inside and clean him up, Wodja. The mill workers will have clothes for him, I am sure."

Phicol assigned several soldiers to stay at the mill to help Wodja. Their task was to guard Samson and make sure he was securely shackled at all times.

Inside the mill, Samson was washed with fresh water. They took off the shackles and dressed him in a short tunic with a long outer robe. Then his hands and feet were bound again with the shackles. The shackles allowed him just enough room to shuffle around. The soldiers then walked him back outside to a small building across the yard of the mill. This building was a low barracks where prisoners who worked at the mill lived. Samson was pushed roughly into one of the rooms and down onto the bed.

"Here are the longer chains, boy," one of the soldiers said to Wodja. "Put them on when he goes out to work. One set will attach to the hand shackles and one to the feet. They are long enough that he will be able to move and work the grinder. This little wrench is to tighten and loosen the screw in the shackles. Watch that they are not too tight, or they will cut off the blood and he will lose his feet and hands like he did his eyes. At night, attach the chains to the bolts in the wall next to the bed."

Wodja took the chains and placed them at the foot of the bed and put the wrench in his pocket.

Samson's room was small, furnished only with a bed, and a little table. Wodja's room was next to Samson's. From there, he brought a chair and placed it at the foot of the bed. The Physician came in and once more applied salve to Samson's eye sockets and replaced the bandage that had been removed. Before long, Phicol came in.

"We are leaving now, Wodja. The physician will come by for the next few days to make sure those wounds do not get infected. In a week, I will be back to see you. The mill supervisor knows what to do with him in the meantime. He will give you instructions."

"Yes, Master Phicol."

Phicol threw a small pouch on the bed. "There is your payment, boy. If you take care of him well, there will be one of those for you each month. This man is very important to me. I think that you understand that already."

"Yes, Master, I do."

"Good. I will see you in one week. I am leaving four men here. Two will be here at all times. They will rotate their time with two here and two resting at the inn up the road. If you need me, they will know how to reach me."

Phicol and his men left, leaving Wodja in the room alone with Samson.

Wodja sat slowly down in the chair. He stared intently at Samson for a long while before he spoke. "Are you in pain, Master Samson?" I can get you some drink to ease the pain."

Samson did not speak. He sat on the bed, straining desperately to see from his empty eye sockets, in spite of the cloths that covered them. His head and chest moved back and forth slowly as if he were rocking himself to sleep.

"Would you like to rest now? You are probably weary from the journey. Would you like me to remove your sandals?"

Still Samson did not speak, but slowly he leaned over and lay down on the bed with his legs hanging over the side and his feet still on the floor.

"I will not hurt you, Master Samson. I promise. I hope you will not hurt me."

Wodja leaned over and unbuckled Samson's sandals from his feet. Then he lifted his feet and placed them on the bed. Samson was already asleep.

The next morning, and every morning for several days, one of Phicol's personal physicians came to the millhouse and tended to Samson. The area around his eye sockets was swollen and red. On the third day, the physician said that some of the tissue inside the eye socket was infected. He offered Samson a drink to dull the pain, but he would not drink. The physician slowly opened the lids and with a tiny knife cut away more of the muscle inside the eye. Again, he washed it out with salt and vinegar water and applied the salve. Wodja could tell that Samson was in pain, but he did not wince or cry out. He had not said a word since arriving at the mill. The physician ordered that Samson not be allowed to work in the mill yet.

Each day, Wodja came into Samson's room with a breakfast of porridge and black bread. Samson would sit up in the bed, and Wodja would place a small tray on his lap. He placed Samson's hands on the food and watched as he slowly picked up the bread and dipped it into the small bowl of porridge. He would eat just a few bites and then stop. Wodja pleaded with him to eat more, but he would not. Wodja would then put a cup of water in his hands, and he would drink.

On the seventh day, early in the morning, Samson heard a loud trumpet blast and the sound of horse's hooves rattling over the cobblestone drive in front of the mill. Wodja came running into the room out of breath.

"It is Commander Phicol. He is back."

Samson said nothing. He sat still on the bed. He could hear Phicol's rough step coming into the room.

"So, Wodja, how is the patient?"

"The physician has reported that he is doing well, Master."

"That is good. Take off those bandages, and let me see."

Wodja moved to the side of the bed. He had no more fear that Samson would hurt him. Gently, he untied the wrapping from Samson's head and wound it around and off. Then he stepped back. Phicol leaned over but not close enough that Samson could reach him if he could see. He took a vial from a pouch at his side, and pulling a cork from its top, he splashed a red liquid onto Samson's legs.

"Yes, he looks fine," Phicol said. "But there is one problem."

"What is it, Master?" Wodja asked.

"I want to see the empty eye sockets. As long as he keeps his eyelids closed, nobody can tell that his eyes are gone. When I bring my guests by to see the mighty Samson on display, I want them to see my handiwork. I do not think I can depend on him to open his eyelids at the proper time. Can I, Samson?"

Samson did not move. He sat on the bed, perfectly still.

"No, I did not think so," Phicol murmured. "Tomorrow, the physician will be sent back, Wodja. His instructions will be to cut off the eyelids completely. I want to be able to look into Samson's soul, right through there." He pointed his finger at Samson's eyelids. "Right through there, Wodja."

Wodja was horrified, but he said nothing. He had only met Commander Phicol on one other occasion, prior to his bringing Samson to the mill. He had come to arrange a contingent of prisoners to work at the mill. Phicol was paid a portion of the mill profits for all of the free labor he provided. However, it was difficult to keep workers there. In chains, they were limited in the work they could do, and without the chains, they ran away. Phicol did not want to keep paying for guards to watch over the workers, but for Samson, he was making an exception. He obviously expected to profit from having Samson there. Now Wodja began to see the true nature of the man. He was inhuman and beastly, and Wodja felt a deep sense of hatred rising up in his heart. In the few days that Samson had been there, Wodja had come to admire him. He suffered his pain and humiliation in silence and never complained. He had asked for nothing. He would rather sit in his room and soil himself than call for someone to bring him the slop pot. He was a man of integrity, and Wodja hated Phicol for what he was going to do to him.

If nothing else, Phicol was a man who meant what he said. The next day, the physician arrived. Wodja escorted him into the room.

"Samson, the physician is here," he called timidly. "You heard what Phicol said yesterday. I am sorry, but I have no choice but to obey his orders unless I want to die. You heard him yourself, your life for my life. The physician has a drink to dull the pain again. Will you drink it?"

Samson lay down on the bed. He crossed his hands over his chest in a sign of submission.

"Will you not drink the draft, Samson? It is going to be very painful."

Samson lay still and said nothing.

The physician approached the bed and leaned over. "I will try not to hurt you, my boy," he said softly. "The pain won't be so bad right now, but later, when the initial shock wears off, it will ache quite badly."

He took a small implement from a little case that he carried with him. It looked like two blades crossing each other. He leaned down and grasped the top eyelid of the right eye between the blades. He pulled and stretched it away from the eye socket. Then, slowly, with a thin knife that was in his other hand, he sliced through the skin as close to the top of the eye socket as he could. Wodja expected the blood to spurt out in a torrent, but it simply gushed down the front and sides of Samson's face.

"Come, boy, dab up the blood," the physician said to Wodja.

Wodja reached beside the physician and held a cloth against Samson's face, gently wiping away the blood. Then the physician repeated the process with the lower lid and the same with the other eye. When he was finished, he had Wodja apply pressure to Samson's face with clean cloths until the bleeding stopped. Then he put on a small amount of salve and wrapped the eye sockets tightly with a band of clean linen.

"I will be back early tomorrow," he said. "I will not rinse and clean it further today. It may start the bleeding again. Tomorrow it will be well clotted, and then we can clean it further." He patted Wodja on the back. "You would be a good physician's assistant," he said. "Maybe I can use you someday, if they ever let you out of this place."

The physician walked out, leaving Wodja and Samson alone.

Wodja sat on the chair next to the bed and watched this unusual man who had come so suddenly into his life. "The physician has left the draft for pain here. Will you drink it now?" he asked.

Samson lay still and did not speak. Tears ran down from Wodja's eyes.

In the days that followed, Samson healed rapidly, and gradually, the pain diminished.

When Phicol returned, he found that Wodja was keeping a cloth wrapped around Samson's eyes, even though they were healed. He grabbed Wodja by the hair and slashed him across the back with the short whip he always carried now.

"You little fool," he shouted at Wodja. "Didn't I tell you that I wanted to see the empty eye sockets? Don't ever let me see him with those rags on his head again. Do you understand?"

"Yes, Master, yes, I do!"

"Tomorrow, the mill master will show you how to shackle him to the grinding wheel. From that day forward, he is to grind wheat every day from dawn to dusk. I will get my money's worth out of him. When I come here, I expect to see him grinding, without bandages hiding his face!"

"Yes, Master. You will."

Samson sat still and listened to this. Although he had not spoken all this time, he had developed an attachment to Wodja. The boy had been kind to him and now the sound of his whipping made Samson's blood boil. However, shackled to his bed and blind there was nothing he could do.

Samson wished that just once Phicol would make the mistake of coming too close to him. He knew his strength from God was gone, but still he was not a weak man. He was quite sure he could choke the life out of Phicol if he could get his hands around his neck. But now that he was recovered, Phicol knew better. He would come close enough to reach Samson with his whip but no closer and was ready in a moment to jump out of harm's way. And every time he came, he repeated his ritual of splashing the red liquid on Samson as if this were some type of religious ceremony.

When Phicol left, Wodja came and sat on his chair next to Samson's bed.

Samson reached up and unwound the bandages from his head. Then he spoke. "What kind of name is Wodja?"

Astounded, a broad grin spread across Wodja's face. "You spoke! You spoke to me!"

"What kind of name is Wodja?" Samson repeated.

"I don't know. The Philistines gave me that name when I was a young boy. They stole me from my home, killed my parents, and gave me that name. I still remember my real name."

"What is it?'

"Zetham."

"Zetham? That is a Hebrew name!"

"Yes, my parents were Israelites."

"Zetham. What tribe is that name from?"

"It is from the tribe of Levi."

"You are a priest!"

"Not everyone in the tribe of Levi is a priest."

"So the Lord God has sent me a priest in my time of trouble. Zetham the priest."

"I am no priest."

Samson reached his hand toward the sound of Zetham's voice. He felt Zetham's legs on the chair and followed his hand up to Zetham's arms and then he grabbed hold of one of his hands. Samson spoke slowly, stretching each word in a low whisper, his voice breaking into sobs between the words. "You have proven yourself a priest to me, Zetham. You have bound my wounds and fed me and cleaned my filth. Does that not sound like a priest to you?"

"I don't know. I have never met a Hebrew priest. Only the priests of Dagon."

"Phhh! They are no priests, just shamans and fakers. If they want to meet a real priest, they can come here, and I will introduce them to Zetham. Zetham the priest of Samson!"

"You certainly went from not talking at all to a flood of words."

They both laughed, and for the first time in many days, a smile came to Samson's face. It was a gruesome, eyeless smile, but it was a smile.

In the days that followed, Samson began his work at the mill. On the first day, he was taken to the millhouse where there was a huge round millstone set in a deep circular trough. Beneath it was a second stone over which the first one turned. A large cloth slide came down from the second floor of the mill and poured the grain beneath the stone. From the center of the upper millstone a large wooden shaft protruded. Attached to the shaft were leather harnesses and metal studs with loops at the top. Into these loops the chains connected to Samson's hand shackles were run and clamped together in the center of the shaft. Wodja hooked Samson onto the shaft and removed the leather harnesses.

"Now, Samson, it is all ready. The shackles are not too tight, are they?"

"No, they are fine."

"When you are ready, just lean against the shaft and push. The millstone will go around in the trough as they pour in the wheat and grind it. Every so often you will stop, and the miller will remove the ground wheat."

"I am ready."

"Then go ahead."

Samson leaned against the shaft and pushed. The stone did not move. He leaned again, groaning and pushing harder. This time the wheel started and then rocked back into place. Samson laughed. "Look, Zetham. Samson the strong man can't push a little wheel in a circle."

"It is not so easy as people think. This stone weighs more than twenty men."

"How many men pushed it before I came?"

"No men at all. It was pulled by a donkey. That is what the leather harnesses I just took off were from."

"A donkey?" Samson gave a loud laugh. "My old friend Phicol does have a sense of humor after all. I cut him with a donkey's jawbone, and he has me replacing a donkey in the mill!" Samson laughed again and then sang, "The donkey in the mill, the donkey in the mill, Samson has now become the donkey in the mill!"

He laughed again, and Zetham laughed with him. Then Samson pushed again, and in a few moments, he had the stone turning. So began his daily work, and it continued in this manner. Every day as the sun rose, Samson started grinding, and as it set, he stopped. In between, he was given periods of rest and time to eat and drink.

One day, Zetham told him that Commander Phicol was coming the following morning. Samson was to be bathed and given a new set of clothes, as Phicol was bringing a group of other army commanders to see Samson, and he wanted Samson to look clean and strong. He sent a special close-fitting tunic with no sleeves for him to wear so Samson's still-impressive arms could be best displayed.

When he rose the next morning, Zetham brought his breakfast, and they sat and talked for a while.

"Will you talk to the commander today?" Zetham asked. "When he was here last, you didn't speak."

"Well, I was still a little distracted by the loss of my eyes."

"So will you speak to him today?"

"If the Lord God gives me anything to say."

When Phicol arrived, he had an even larger group with him than previously. At least a thousand men lined the road leading up to the mill. Horns sounded as each commander rode into the mill yard at the head of his troop. When they had all dismounted, Phicol led a group of his top twenty-five men into the mill where Samson was grinding.

"There he is, gentlemen. The mighty Samson, here at our beck and call to grind for us as we please. Isn't he magnificent?"

The other commanders gave their assent by clapping rhythmically and shouting, "Hail, Lord Phicol, conqueror of Samson!"

Then Phicol called out in a loud voice, "Stop grinding, Samson!"

Samson stopped and stood still, holding his hands on the post.

"Do you see his lovely eyes, men? Or let me phrase it better. Do you see where they once were? Taken out by my own hands!"

Again, the commanders clapped and shouted.

"How are you today, Samson?" Phicol asked.

Samson said nothing.

"Samson, I am talking to you," Phicol yelled. "I asked how you are."

Samson was still silent.

"Well, perhaps I can loosen your tongue," Phicol said. "Samson, you might remember my whip. I have always liked to have one with me. I am quite good at using it, but I thought it inadequate for a foe such as you, so I had another one custom made with you in mind. It is a bit longer and very stiff. The edges of the leather have been ground very thin so they are quite sharp, like the edge of a knife. I have tested it out on several men. It works rather well. I did not want to use it on you today and ruin your nice new clothes and embarrass you in front of all these noble commanders. However, I will do so, if you insist. So I will ask you one more time." Now Phicol's voice dropped to a menacing whisper. "How are you today, Samson?"

Samson said nothing. Phicol stepped forward to within a few feet of the end of the wooden shaft that Samson was leaning against. He took the vial he always carried in a pouch at his waist and, as he had before, splashed the red fluid on Samson's hands. Then the whip lashed out, hitting Samson across the chest. The new tunic tore, revealing a red line of blood beneath.

"How are you today, Samson?" Phicol repeated.

Again, Samson was silent.

The whip went out again and again, slashing Samson's arms and face until blood flowed across the front of his body. Phicol stepped back, breathing heavily.

"You've got me all out of breath, Samson. How are you today?"

Samson stood and said nothing.

Phicol resumed the whipping, cutting now one way and then across the other. Samson's face was bloodied, and his arms and legs were covered with long welts and cuts. Finally, he went down to his knees, and Phicol laughed.

"Look, my friends, how the mighty Samson falls to his knees before me. Never will you see a sight like this again in your lives. The mighty man of Israel who carried the gates of a city on his shoulders, tore lions to pieces, and killed countless of our fellow soldiers! Here he is. Who else would like to take the whip to him?"

Several of the commanders came forward and took the whip in their hands. They, too, slashed and cut.

"Do not get too close now, Seton!" Phicol laughed. "He is bowed, but he might still have a bite or two left in him."

Before long, they all tired of this sport. Samson was slumped down on the ground, blood running from all over his body, his wrists still chained to the turn post of the grinding stone.

"We will leave you now, Samson," Phicol called as he and the others turned to go. "Maybe the next time we come you will have a word or two for us. Good-bye, old friend, and thank you. We have not had so much fun since our last raid on the people of Israel. In fact, they were not near as much fun as you. They just died! Ha ha ha! Good-bye, Samson."

"Good-bye, Samson!" the other commanders echoed.

When they were gone, Zetham rushed forward and quickly undid the shackles on Samson's hands and feet. He was unconscious on the ground. Zetham ran and got the miller, who had wisely stayed upstairs in the grain room. Together, they managed to lift Samson onto one of the grain carts and roll it over to his room. The two Philistine guards on duty refused to help them.

With great effort, Zetham and the miller hoisted Samson up and got him onto the bed. Zetham brought clean cloths and a bucket of water and began to bathe his wounds. The physician had left some of the salve he had used on Samson's eyes, and Zetham applied this to the more serious cuts. Then he slowly wrapped strips of cloth around Samson's arms and legs. He sobbed softly as he worked. There was little area across the front of Samson's body that was not cut or bruised. When Zetham was almost finished, Samson regained consciousness.

"Is that you, Zetham?"

"Yes, Samson. It is I."

"What is all over me?"

"Keep still. They are bandages. Those beasts cut you up pretty badly."

"I guess Phicol doesn't like the strong silent type, eh?"

"Ah Samson. You make jokes even when they almost killed you."

"What else would you have me do, Zetham, cry and moan?"

"No, I guess the jokes are better. Let me get you a drink."

Zetham left and came back with a cup of water and a few slices of bread dipped in oil. "Here, eat this. You lost a lot of blood. You need to get your strength back. I don't think the miller will expect you at the wheel for a few days."

"I hope he kept the donkey," Samson said, chewing a piece of bread. Zetham laughed.

As he had before, Samson healed quickly. For the first few days after Phicol's visit, he stayed in bed, barely able to move from the pain. Phicol sent the physician, who bathed the wounds and applied more salve. The physician was not a bad man, and Samson had actually come to like him. He made jokes with him as he applied the bandages.

"So, Doctor Philistine, have you ever seen your fellow Philistines spend so much time and money keeping one of their enemies alive?" Samson laughed.

"No, I have not," the Doctor chuckled. "But then I have never known them to capture an enemy like you. That is, if half of what they say about you is true."

"And what do they say about me?"

"They say that you killed a thousand men with your bare hands, tore a full-grown lion in half, and carried the gates of a city on your shoulders. They make you sound like some type of god."

"Well, you know better than that, don't you? No god would be lying here with his eyes gouged out and cut to ribbons. At least no god I would want to worship."

"That is another thing they say. That you betrayed your god and he abandoned you."

"Yes? Well, part of that is true, I did betray my God. But He has not abandoned me. He is still watching over me. Am I not alive? What other man would still be alive in these circumstances?"

"You are quite right. I don't know anyone else who would be alive under the hands of Commander Phicol. I have sewn up and bandaged many of his men but never one of his enemies. They were left in the hands of others who used knives, but not as I use them. No, there is no doubt you are unique, Master Samson."

"Why do you call me Master? I am not your master."

"It is a sign of respect. You have proved yourself to be a man of honor. You could easily have grabbed and killed me many times while I was here. I am an old man. I could not resist much. The other enemies of the Philistines would not have hesitated to wrap those chains around my neck and choke me to death."

"Only a fool would kill a man who was trying to heal him."

"There are many fools in the world, Samson. Many fools."

For days afterward, Samson could hardly turn over in bed, as every move touched a raw nerve or sore spot. When he could walk again, Zetham would take him every few days down by the sea along the coastal road. The guards came with them, walking many yards behind them. They allowed Samson to go with only the shackles on his hands and none on his feet. On one of these walks, they stood on a bluff overlooking the sea. Samson turned his head up to the sky and breathed in deeply.

"Smell that air, Zetham?" he said. "It is the most wonderful smell in the world. The smell of the sea."

"Yes, I like it too. I used to come here often in the evening when I had nothing to do before you came."

"You would have been better off if I had never come. I am sorry that I have brought you so much trouble and work, taking care of an old, blind man."

"You are not old."

"I am old enough, Zetham. I have been a judge in Israel for almost twenty years now. My father is past seventy years, if he is still alive."

"When did you see your parents last?"

"Just before I was captured. I had sent them away for a long time to keep them far from Phicol. Then I let them come back home. I am sorry I did now. You heard what Phicol said. I don't think he will bother them as long as he has me under his heel, but with him you can never be sure. I pay hundreds of men to guard over their home, but still I worry."

"How did you become a judge, Samson?"

"It is a long story. The story of my life, really."

"We have time."

Samson told Zetham all about his life, starting with the visit from the Angel of the Lord and all the events that led to his capture by Phicol.

"I suppose I have wasted my life, Zetham. The angel told my mother that God would begin to deliver our people from the Philistines through me. I can't imagine that happening now, now that I am here, eyeless in Gaza. I thought I saw things clearly before, but even though I had eyes and could see, I was blind. They took my eyes, and **then** I saw. I saw what a fool I was, full of pride and my own desires. Now God has left me to die here among my enemies, a disgrace to my people."

"You are not a disgrace, Samson. The people of Israel love you and will remember you for all you did before you came here."

"You are kind, Zetham. I can only hope so. Anyway, I should not complain. I have had adventures that other men would give everything they own to have had. I once raced a gazelle from our eastern border almost to the sea. When he tired, I carried him on my shoulders. I stood on the crest of a hill in the land of Judah and saw a ship whipped by the winds, about to be washed onto the rocks. I raced down the hill, dove into the icy waters, swam as fast as a dolphin to the ship, and jumped on board like a whale that breaches the sea. I grabbed the massive ropes used for mooring the ship, wrapped them around me, dove back into the water, and pulled the ship to the shore safely. Not a single sailor was lost that day. The men kissed my hands and bowed down to me like I was a god. I have seen things other men can only dream of, Zetham. There is still much that I wanted to do. I have always wanted to follow the sun for one day from the moment it peeps above the horizon in the east until it sags down to the land in the west, to stay perpetually in its warm radiance and follow it to the place where it, too, must sleep. I have wished to soar like an eagle the way I pretended to when I was a boy, high above the world, where nothing can touch you." Samson paused. "Yes, perhaps the people of Israel will remember me kindly. I can only hope so."

"Did you say your wife's name was Merari?" Zetham asked.

"Yes. Why?"

"That is a Hebrew name also."

"Yes, it is. I thought it was a name for a man. Her mother was a Hebrew."

"But, Samson, Merari was one of the sons of Levi!"

"Another priest or priestess? I guess God has been sending me priests for some time now. Next you will tell me that Delilah was a cousin to the tribe of Levi."

"No, I guess we will just have to leave her as an Egyptian. Anyway, the people of Israel spent a long time in Egypt. I am sure many of them had Egyptian wives and concubines also."

"I guess so, Zetham. I guess so. I have a favor to ask you."

"What is it? You just have to ask."

"I have composed a song, and I want you to write it down for me. Someday I hope you can escape from here. If you do, I want you to find my mother and father in the territory of Dan and give them this song and tell them that I love them dearly."

"Maybe we can both escape and you can sing the song for them yourself."

"I don't think so, Zetham. A young man and an old, blind man would not get far here so deep in the land of the Philistines. Phicol would be after us in a moment. No, this is a task just for you, my priest."

"I will do it, Samson. But first I must tell you that I will make no attempt to escape as long as you are alive and here. I will not leave you alone, ever."

"The faithful priest to the end. Alright, Zetham. You are young. I just ask the Lord God to set you free before my parents are dead."

"He will answer your prayer. I am sure of it. Now what about the song?"

"You don't have any parchment or way to write it down."
"I have a very good memory. Sing it to me."
Samson pointed his face to the sky and slowly, softly sang.

"I once walked bold like a man alone,
who thinks that he'll never fall.
And then I awoke with a mighty groan,
Just to find I was nothing at all.

"Oh Lord, dear Lord, You're the mighty King.
Oh Lord, dear Lord, hear my plea.
You are master and ruler of everything,
And I pray that You'll please pardon me.

"How dark and cold is the pit of hell,
Into which I plunged my poor soul.
And how I walked in that wretched well,
With a heart that was blackened as coal.

"Oh Lord, dear Lord, You're the mighty King.
Oh Lord, dear Lord, hear my plea.
You are master and ruler of everything,
And I pray that You'll please pardon me.

"But now I walk with a humble heart,
Before Your great throne where I sing,
Of the great I AM who still stands apart,
From the world because He is its King.

Oh Lord, dear Lord, You're the mighty King.
Oh Lord, dear Lord, hear my plea.
You are master and ruler of everything,

And I pray that You'll please pardon me."

Zetham was silent for a long time after Samson finished singing.

"Are you there, Zetham? Did I put you to sleep?"

"No, I am here. That was beautiful."

"Will you remember it all?"

"Yes, I will remember. Later, I will write it down. I will never forget that song, Samson."

"Good. You are a faithful priest."

PHICOL: THE GENERAL

P hicol did not come to the mill for two years after the visit in which Samson was so savagely beaten. From time to time, he sent groups of people with some of the other commanders to see Samson, but Phicol did not come.

A constant stream of travelers came along the highway running north from Gaza, many stopping at the mill to see the mighty Samson. Throughout the land of Philistia, along all its far-flung borders, the word had spread. "Samson, the hero of Israel, is in bondage in Gaza. Come see him grinding at the mill. For one piece of gold, you can witness how low Samson has been hurled down by Commander Phicol. He is reduced to slavery, making bread for our kitchens."

People came in droves. A special rail had to be constructed around the path that Samson trod each day to keep back the gawkers. If it were not for the soldiers who were still stationed there permanently, they would have pushed through to tear off a piece of Samson's garment or snatch a lock of his hair. More soldiers had to be sent to stay at the mill to keep the crowds under control, to collect the money, and to screen all the visitors for spies. Nobody was allowed to touch or talk to Samson. The income from the spectators now far outstripped what the mill itself produced. Phicol's investment was paying off well.

Samson's hair had grown back. He wondered about this and spoke of it to Zetham. "Why have they not cut my hair, Zetham? Do they not know it was the source of my strength? I have felt my strength returning. The millstone has become like a feather."

"Yes, I have noticed how much easier it is for you to get started in the morning. I do not believe they know about your hair. I have heard the soldiers talking. They said whenever I am close to you I should sprinkle wine on you, and you would become weak and not be able to hurt me. That must be what Phicol is doing when he comes and splashes the liquid from his little bottle on you. Anyway, you said it was your vow before God that was the source of your strength, not your hair."

"Yes, that is true. But the hair was a symbol of my faithfulness to the vow. I will need you to braid it for me. My mother taught me to do it when I was a child, but it is hard now that I cannot see. Perhaps it would be best to tie the braids in the back and wear a cloth over them while I am grinding. The less attention I draw to them the better."

"I will take care of it. Do not worry."

"You say they said to sprinkle wine on me? I wonder where they got that idea."

A few days later, Zetham came in very early in the morning. "Samson, get up. The soldiers awoke me early today and said to get you ready. Commander Phicol is coming again."

"Ah, I guess I better get ready for the whip."

"Can you not just talk to him this time? Would that be so hard?"

"Are you afraid for me, Zetham? Do not fret yourself. If I am to die under Phicol's whip, I will die. It will only end the torment of living in this darkness."

"Well, you better get up. He wants you bathed and dressed when he gets here."

"I don't know why Phicol goes to so much trouble to clean me up just so he can get me all bloody and dirty again."

"Not this time, Samson. I beg you, not this time. Just say a simple word to him."

"For your sake, Zetham? Yes, yes, I will. For your sake."

Within an hour, Samson heard the trumpets and the scuffle of the horses coming into the mill yard. Phicol entered his room and called Zetham to him.

"Bring me a larger chair, boy. I will sit this time."

Zetham ran to the millhouse and got one of the large chairs from the dining table of the miller and put it at the foot of Samson's bed. Samson sat on the bed, still and quiet. One of the soldiers walked over to him and poured a small amount of wine across his neck.

"Now, Samson," Phicol began. "I have come to express my gratitude to you. This day I am elevated to the greatest position in Philistia. I am now the Supreme General of all the Philistine forces, and I have you to thank for it."

"You are welcome," Samson said.

"Oh, you are talking!" Phicol replied with a laugh. "That is good, Samson. So we did learn something last time. Good, good. That makes me very happy. There are good things in store for you, Samson. There is no need for us to be enemies any longer. I want to help you as you have helped me. I am going to give you the opportunity to earn your freedom from this mill!"

"That sounds very generous of you. What will I have to do to earn it?"

"Almost nothing. Just behave yourself and act like a good slave in front of the commanders. There is a great feast and celebration of my promotion planned for thirty days from now. It will take place in the temple of Dagon here in Gaza. It is going to be the greatest gathering of the Philistines that has ever taken place. Every governor, commander, and leader that we have will be there, several thousand people. The talk among the governors is that they wish to declare me as king of the Philistines. We have never had a king before. It is a title they would only be willing to bestow on a man who could defeat the mighty Samson. You will be there also, if you agree to my terms."

"What terms?"

"You will be chained between the mighty pillars of the temple. The lords of the Philistines will pass by to see you. You will treat them with respect and deference and dance and frolic in front of them. You will act as though you yourself have been treated like a king. We want the world to hear of the mercy of the Philistines. We are not barbaric, as it has been said. We treat our prisoners with kindness. Could I not have killed you long ago?"

"There was more profit in keeping me alive."

"Yes, that is true. But that is not the reason that I did. This feast is the reason, Samson. All of the whippings were just to help prepare you for this day. Now, in talking to me in this logical fashion, you have shown me that you are ready. Do you realize how famous you are? Among our people your name is second only to mine. Everyone in the country wants to see you. Many of our women have expressed a desire to marry you and raise up a new flock of heroes for our people."

"Half breeds? I thought your people frowned on that."

"Normally, yes. But in your case, they are willing to make an exception. They are calling you a god, Samson! Imagine that. Some have even suggested that I bring my wife to breed with you. I could be father to your son. Wouldn't that be something?"

"Yes," Samson chuckled and replied slowly. "That would be something."

"Listen to me, Samson. This feast is very important to me. If you perform well, I will personally guarantee that you will be set free from the mill. You will never have to grind here again. We were enemies for a long time, but there is no profit in that now. I am sure your priest Zetham here will agree with me, won't you, Zetham?"

Samson lifted his head at the mention of the name Zetham.

"Oh yes, Samson, I know all about Wodja being Zetham, your secret priest. The miller is a faithful and fearful servant of mine. He has big ears and has told me about your conversations with my little Wodja. If I had known he was a priest, I might have used his services myself. I have my household gods to be tended to also. Now, what is your answer? Will you behave and perform nicely for us?"

"I will come to your feast. I will dance and even sing if you like. I ask nothing in return except one thing."

"What is that?"

"You will set Zetham free. Send him back to the land of my fathers and have him send a message back to me that he is safe."

"It is agreed. I would give you my hand on the matter, but I am not so foolish as that yet. You know my word, Samson. I have always tried to do what I said I would do."

"I will trust your word, Phicol."

"Good, then it is settled. You will do no more grinding here. The shackles will be taken off for now, although on the day of the feast you will be bound between the columns with chains. I am sending my personal physician to stay with you until the feast. He will make sure that you have no open wounds or sores. He will oil your skin and take you out in the sun every day. I want you to look your most magnificent on the day of the feast. Oh, and about the breeding matter. Perhaps you thought I was jesting. I was not. Some of the commanders are quite serious about it. They would pay a king's ransom to have you service their wives and provide them a god for a son."

"That is not likely to happen, Phicol."

"No? Well, that is a shame. It would not have been an unpleasant experience for you, I think. You used to like being with the women quite a bit, but I could understand if the last time left you a bit hesitant. Well, good-bye, Samson. I will not see you again until the day of the feast. I look forward to it. You, Zetham, come here."

Zetham had been standing in the doorway, listening to the conversation. He approached Phicol and stood in front of him.

"Zetham, you have heard what was said here."

"Yes, General. I heard."

"You have my word that when the feast is over, you will be given safe escort into the territory of Israel. You may devise whatever code you wish to send a special message back to Samson to let him know you are safe. Be prepared to leave when the feast is over."

"I do not wish to leave Samson, General. What will happen to him afterward?"

"I do not know. An auction has been suggested to sell him to the highest bidder. I am already a rich man, but they say this auction would make me wealthy beyond my wildest dreams. Perhaps even as wealthy as Samson's father, and that is very wealthy. Samson asks nothing for himself. He asks only for you to be set free. That I have granted. Beyond that, we will see."

"Yes, General. Can I stay with him if I wish?"

"You will have to work that out with him. If he approves it, and we still have a bargain, yes."

"Thank you, General."

When Phicol had left, Zetham stood in the doorway watching his procession recede down the road.

"Are you there, Zetham?" Samson asked, still sitting on his bed.

"I am here."

"Did you hear that? God has answered my prayer. You are going to be free. You will go to live with my family. They are wealthy, Zetham. I have told you that, and you heard Phicol confirm it. They will take good care of you."

Zetham began to cry. "Do you think I would leave you?" he sobbed. He walked over to the bed where Samson was sitting and hugged Samson's head to him, his chest heaving.

Samson put his arms around Zetham's waist and hugged him. He turned his face up to Zetham and said in a whisper, "You must go, Zetham! You must. Don't you know what joy it would bring me to know you are free and safe? You could take care of my mother and father for me. I will never be able to do that now, Zetham. You must!"

"Why couldn't you let him give you your freedom? It sounded like he would if you had asked!"

"You have to know how to listen to Phicol, Zetham. He said he would set me free from the mill, but he is not about to let me go completely. Even a blind man might lead a rebellion against the Philistines. He will not let that happen. That talk of an auction was foolishness. He is not about to let me out from under his thumb. If they plan a great celebration in their temple, they must have great sacrifices for their god also. What greater sacrifice than Samson?"

"Why do you say that? He sounds like he wants peace with you."

"There is no real peace with the Philistines, Zetham. That is one thing I have learned. In many respects, our priests were right. We cannot compromise with these people. When we do, we invite in their gods and their ways and we lose our land. Every year that we let them, they push farther north into Israel. That has been so since Joshua brought the people across the Jordan and settled the land. Every square mile the people of Israel have captured, the Philistines have contested and tried to steal. I do not think that will ever change."

"How can you ask me to leave you, Samson? We are like brothers now. I cannot leave!"

"Yes, Zetham, you can and you will for the very reason you just stated. We are brothers now. This brother cannot go home again. But you can. As my brother, you can return to Zorah and care for our parents. They will love you and treat you as they treated me. You will do this for me, Zetham. God has answered my prayer, and you will not want to be the person who thwarts His will."

"No, Samson. I would not want to thwart the will of holy God."

"Then it is settled. The code will be simple. Is there anyone else here with us?"

"No, we are alone. The soldiers went into the millhouse to eat their breakfast."

"The code you will send back to me is this: the new young eagle has arrived."

"I remember the story you told of when you were a boy with your father. I will not forget. The new young eagle has arrived. Aww, Aww, Aww!"

Samson laughed. "Aww, aww, aww!" he cried.

SAMSON: THE MAN OF GOD

For the following weeks, Samson was treated like royalty. Phicol sent special food for him to eat, dates and figs and sweet cakes. He no longer pushed the grinding wheel. The physician came and checked all of his wounds. Some had indeed festered, in spite of Zetham's careful tending. These he cut into with his tiny knife to release pus and fluid that had built up in them. Then he swabbed them with his special salve and put clean bandages on them every day. Samson sat in the sun for an hour each morning, wearing only his loincloth. His body grew stronger and a deeper shade of bronze as the weeks passed. Every night, Zetham bathed him and anointed him with the special oils Phicol had sent and carefully washed and braided the seven braids of his hair, which had fully grown back now.

Phicol had sent a tailor to measure Samson and produce several new sets of clothes, tunics and robes with golden hems. One set of clothes was specifically for the feast. It consisted of a short tunic that came down between Samson's knees and his loins. Attached to the back of the tunic was a long cape of bright red linen, embroidered all around the border with silver thread. There were also boots of fine leather. They were black with gold filaments stitched into the front. The boots came halfway up Samson's leg between the ankle and the knee. Phicol had sent a cobbler to measure Samson's feet and custom make the boots. All of this was delivered with great fanfare and the sound of trumpets.

Finally, the day of the feast arrived. A special chariot was sent to pick up Samson and Zetham. The plain shackles and chains had been replaced with ones made of polished bronze. Zetham sat in the chariot and looked at Samson, dressed in the tunic and cape. He looked magnificent.

When they arrived at the temple, Samson was taken to the center of the first floor. There, two huge columns stood close together. His chains were wrapped around the two columns and then firmly fixed together with a large golden lock.

Zetham described the temple to him in a hushed voice. "It is huge, Samson. There are people everywhere."

"How many floors are there?"

"Three. This one, another above us where they said the banquet tables are set up, and another above that. There are stairs all around, leading up to those floors."

"Are there tables for sitting on this floor?"

"No. There is an altar at the far end with a statue. I suppose that is Dagon. The rest of this floor is an open courtyard."

"Put my hands on the pillars so I can feel them and lean against them."

Zetham took Samson's right hand and placed it against one of the pillars. Then he took the left hand and placed it on the other. Samson felt the smooth marble on his palms. He turned his head up and smiled.

"All right, Zetham. We are ready now. Remember where you are going when this is over."

"Yes, I remember."

Before long, trumpets were blowing around the temple and a great shout went up. "Make way for General Phicol, lord of the Philistines!"

A long, golden chariot was driven right onto the floor of the temple. When it got to the center, Phicol stepped down. He was dressed in a robe from his neck to his feet made entirely of gold thread and embedded with precious jewels, which shone and glittered as he walked. A priest of Dagon got down from the chariot behind him and led him to the altar at the far end of the room.

Phicol raised his hands in front of the altar and cried out in a loud voice, "Hail, Dagon. We are gathered here in front of you, the rulers of Ashkelon, Gaza, Ashdod, Ekron, and Gath. We come to bring you praise!"

There were six small children standing around the altar. The priest took one by the hand and led him over to stand next to Phicol. Phicol lifted the child and placed him on the altar in front of him. He pulled a small dagger from beneath his cloak and quickly sliced across the child's neck. A great shout went up throughout the temple. "Hail, Dagon!"

Zetham was horrified. He had never witnessed the rituals of the Philistines in their temples. He cringed when he saw the little child's blood running down the sides of the altar and his body twitching in the throes of death. Another priest approached and spread a large white linen cloth in front of the altar so Phicol would not soil his boots in the blood.

One by one, the other children were brought to Phicol. They moved slowly as though they were dazed and did not know what was happening to them. When Zetham told Samson what was going on, Samson commented that he hoped it was because they had been drugged beforehand. Still, it hurt him to hear Zetham describe the slaughter. His mind burned with the desire to destroy these people who could so callously kill a little child. It would not have surprised him to know that the first child had been Phicol's own son.

Before long, it was over. Phicol came across the polished marble floor toward Samson. In a loud voice, he proclaimed, "Look here, people of Philistia. Our once-great enemy Samson is here. Our god has delivered our enemy into our hands!"

The entire hall erupted as the Philistines chanted, "Our god has delivered our enemy into our hands!"

The temple was filled with people now, and they continued streaming in from all sides as latecomers arrived.

"Yes, my friends," Phicol continued. "The mighty Samson is here. He has been defeated by the forces of my army, and his eyes were gouged out by my own hand. He will dance for us here today. He will dance to the tune of the Philistines!"

With that, some musicians who had gathered in a small roped-off area behind Samson began playing a tune. They had harps, flutes, drums, and other instruments and played with wild abandon. Several women in flowing robes came and danced around Samson.

"Now dance for us, Samson!" Phicol shouted.

Samson began to dance, slowly at first and then faster and faster and with greater abandon. His chains kept him in a confined space, but in that space, he whirled around until the chains were wrapped tightly around him, and then he whirled the other way. He repeated this twirling dance several times. In his mind, he was thinking, *Yes, Phicol, this will be my dance of death for you.* He was quite certain that Phicol planned to kill him at the end of the feast. If children were valuable as sacrifices to Dagon, how much more so the mighty Samson. While he danced, the Philistines clapped and laughed and shouted, "Hail to Samson, the dancer of Israel! Hail to Phicol, the greatest of all generals who defeated him!"

Soon, Phicol signaled to the headwaiter of the temple and raised his voice above the music. "We will now serve you, my lords and ladies. If you will make your way to the second floor, the tables are set and waiting for you."

One by one, they left the hall and ascended the stairs. Phicol stayed back near Samson.

"I am very proud of you, Samson," he said. "You have kept your word, and I will keep mine. Zetham will leave here a free man today."

"Thank you, General," Samson responded. "I am grateful to you."

"By the way, you dance very well for a Hebrew. They are not known for their dancing skill."

"Thank you, General. Would you like to have a little dance with me? We could take off the chains and dance all around the hall. You would have to lead the way, of course, since I cannot see."

"Ha ha ha! I am glad you have not lost your sense of humor, Samson. Maybe some other time." Phicol left and walked up the stairs to the second floor banquet.

"Are you here, Zetham?" Samson asked.

"I am here, Samson. They have sent food for you."

"No, Zetham. I will not eat anything served in this temple, and neither should you."

"I did not plan to."

"Have they all gone?"

"Most of them. Some are still arriving, I suppose. I see more chariots coming."

"How many soldiers are stationed outside?"

"Hardly any now. They all came in and went up to eat. They have special tables for them on the third floor. There are still some servants outside directing people in and taking their chariots and horses to the corral they have set up down the road."

Samson reached out and touched the two pillars again. "Are there other pillars besides these in the temple, Zetham?"

"Yes."

"Where are they?"

"There are pillars all around the outer fringe of the temple. These are the only two in the middle."

"Ah, this is a good place to rest." Samson sat down on the floor.

As the day wore on and more people arrived, they came one by one and looked at Samson. Soon, the stream of onlookers stopped, and Samson was alone with Zetham.

After several hours had passed, Zetham was called away by one of the kitchen servants. He was gone for several minutes and then returned. He stood behind one of the huge columns. There was nobody else on the first floor now. The revelry up above was like most Philistine feasts, with huge volumes of wine and spirits flowing. They would all be drunk before the day was gone. Zetham whispered to Samson who had lain down and fallen asleep. "Samson, Samson."

"Yes, Zetham, I am here." Samson sat up and then stood. "What is wrong?"

"Nothing. But there is someone here to see you."

"Who is it?"

From behind the column, Samson heard a voice, a tiny, sweet voice that played like music in his ears. It was the voice of his mother. "Samson, my son."

"Mother, what are you doing here?" Samson asked, barely able to stifle his voice and his emotions.

"I am working in the kitchen, helping to cook the food."

"But how, Mother? How did you get here?"

"The word of your captivity reached us a long time ago, my son. Your father and I thought to contact the Philistines and see if they would let us buy your freedom. We sent envoys, but they would not hear of it. We tried to come and see you at the mill, but they were checking everyone who they did not know. Men who were not known to them were checked to see if they were circumcised or not. We knew we could never get in."

"Oh Mother, for the sake of holy God, why did you come here?"

"I had to see my son, my only son."

With that, Samson broke out in sobs that wrenched the heart of his mother. She touched his hand where it rested against one of the columns.

"Shh. There, there, my son. Do not cry. It is alright. When your father and I heard of the plans for this great feast, we put on our best peasant clothes and came here. They were desperate for good cooks and workers in the kitchen, and they hired us right away. It has been many years since your father worked for wages. Even at the age of seventy-five, he can still work hard."

"Where is he, Mother?"

"He is in the kitchen. He was hired to mop the floor and clean up after the feast. We did not think it wise to both come out here at the same time. We saw this young man from the kitchen, and we thought we could trust him."

"Yes, Mother, you can. This is Zetham, my brother and my priest."

Zelponi turned to look kindly at Zetham, who was standing beside her behind the column out of view of any who might pass in front of Samson. They need not have worried. None of the Philistines liked to leave the table once the drinking and eating had begun.

"Mother, you have to leave this place. You must go back to Zorah quickly. You can take Zetham with you. Phicol has promised to free him, but I do not trust his word a bit. You must leave, Mother."

"Samson, if I died today, I would die a happy woman. God has allowed me once more to put my eyes on my son. You are the apple of these eyes, and if I could give them to you, I would gladly do it."

Samson began to sob again. Tears came from the corners of his eye sockets and rolled down his face.

"Now, now, my boy, hush, hush." Zelponi said softly. "Everything is alright. Do not cry. I am here with you."

"Mother, I love you. How can I ever thank you for the life you gave me? You and Father were like God to me. But now, you have to leave here. You must do one last thing for me."

"What is it, Son?"

"When you go back to the kitchen, get a small pot and a spoon. Then you and Father leave. Tell the people in the kitchen that Father has gotten sick and vomited. Tell them that you do not want to contaminate the food with his presence. Then go outside. Zetham said there is a road that runs away from the temple and leads to a corral for the horses and chariots. Go to the corral. When you get there, tap on the pot like you used to do when you would call me for dinner. Do it loud so I can hear. Then Zetham will join you. He will help you get a chariot and escape. Promise me you will do this."

"I will do it, my son. I promise. What about you, my darling? What will they do to you? Will they kill you?"

"I think so, Mother. I am certain that Phicol plans a grand finale for his feast. What better way to end it than to make a sacrifice to Dagon of the mighty Samson? But it is alright, Mother. My Lord and my God is with me."

"I know He is with you, my darling son."

Zelponi started to sob. She came out from behind the column and stood in front of Samson and hugged him around the waist. He reached down and kissed her head. With his arms around her, he could feel her body shaking. She looked up into his face. With her fingertip she slowly traced a line around the sockets of his eyes. Then she traced the lines on his face, the scars from Phicol's whip.

"My son, my son, my darling son," she sobbed. "What have they done to you? I love you more than my life. I would stay here and die with you."

Samson took her hand and kissed it. Then he whispered.

"No, Mother. This is my time now. My time to finish what God started in my life. I have shackles on my hands now, but God has taken the shackles off of my heart. I have peace in my heart about what will happen here today. My greatest regret is the pain I have caused you and Father, the two people I love most in the world. It was the strength of yours and Father's convictions that gave me my strength. Now you will go, and in your heart, I will go with you and will be there with you forever. Now go, before they see you."

Samson kissed the top of her head, and she kissed his chest and arms. Then Zetham led her away, crying as she went.

Samson fell to his knees and cried. He did all he could to hold back the sobs, as he did not want the Philistines to hear. His heart was racked with pain, and his mind blazed with fear that his mother and father would fall into Phicol's hands.

After a few minutes, Zetham called out again. "Samson."

Samson stood up and stepped back, closer to the column. From behind, he heard another voice that shot into his mind like an arrow. With the sound of that voice, a thousand memories flooded through his head.

"Samson, my son."

"Father, is it really you, come to me like the angel came to you that day?"

"I am no angel, my son, but I have come. The hordes of a thousand Philistines could not keep me away from my son in his hour of need."

Manoah now reached out and touched the hand of his son. Samson felt along his fingers and up to his palm and his wrist.

"How I loved to touch your hands when I was a boy, Father. The hands that could forge metal into swords and still lift me up like a soft carpet into the sky. My eagle father."

"Aww, aww, aww!" Manoah whispered softly.

"Aww, aww aww!" Samson responded.

"Aww, aww, aww!" Zetham echoed from behind the column.

"Father, you have to leave now. They may be back down anytime to gawk at me again. You must leave. I have told Mother what to do. She will tell you when you get back to the kitchen."

"She has told me already. I have some food here to smear on my mouth when I go back so I can feign being sick. I do not want to leave you, my son, here among the Philistines. I would rather die here with you."

"No, Father. You must get Mother away from here. Do not worry about me. There is not much more they can do to me. I will be fine. Zetham will go with you. He has been like a brother to me."

"I heard. You have already trained him in the ways of the eagle."

"Yes, he will be a good eagle for you. Now go, Father, before they come."

Manoah gripped Samson's hand once more. Tears filled his eyes, but he controlled his voice. "I love you, my son. I have always been proud of you but never more than today. In spite of all they have done to you, you stand tall for the Lord God. He will reward you."

"He already did, Father. Years ago, when he gave you to me as my father. What else could I have asked for?"

"God bless and go with you, my son."

"God bless you, Father."

Manoah held Samson's hand and kissed it, and then he followed Zetham back to the kitchen. Soon, Zetham returned.

"They are gone, Samson. When they saw your father with the food smeared all over his tunic, they sent them away quickly. They do not want the wrath of Phicol to come on them if he found they served him tainted food from a sick worker."

"Thank you, Zetham. Now it is your turn to leave."

"Not yet, Samson. We have to make sure they are well away from here before I go. Even now some of the Philistines are coming down the stairs. It is Phicol!" Zetham backed away from Samson and stood behind the column. Samson quickly wiped the tears from his face.

Phicol came up to Samson, leading a tall lady on his arm.

"Samson, my boy. We have a special guest here. She has come back to visit us after a long absence."

Samson lifted his head and sniffed the air.

"Ah, you recognize her perfume. Attar of roses, isn't it, my darling? I remember it well. I am sure Samson does, too, although he might wish to forget the last time he smelled it. Yes, Samson, it is your dear

Delilah, come back to visit us. She says she has been sojourning in Egypt, enjoying her wealth, no doubt. Say hello, Delilah."

"Hello, Samson," Delilah said softly.

Samson was silent.

"Oh no, Samson," Phicol said with mock sorrow in his voice. "Not the silent treatment again. Your love came to visit you! Surely you can at least greet her."

Samson said nothing.

"Well, maybe he is intimidated by my being here, Delilah. You remember what a shy lover he was. He prefers his lovemaking in private. I will leave you with him. Maybe then he will speak." Phicol turned to walk away but then turned back. "Oh Delilah, I would not get too close if I were you. We don't need any more sacrifices down here just yet."

"Will you not speak to me, Samson?" Delilah asked when Phicol was gone. Zetham watched warily from his position behind the column.

"What do you want me to say?" Samson responded.

"That you forgive me! I had no idea what they would do to you, Samson. I am sorry."

"What did you think Phicol would do? Kiss me? I guess his kisses would have been better than yours. He never pretended to be anything but my enemy."

"I deserved that. But at least I did not totally betray you."

"What do you mean by that?"

"I never told them your secret, Samson. I lied to them. Why do you think they have allowed your hair to grow back? Do you not think Phicol would shave your head every day if he knew it was connected to your strength? I lied to them. I told them it was the drinking of wine that would weaken you. I told them I would entice you to drink wine and you would become weak. I said cutting your hair would just prove you were in my power. And they believed me. I also said that just touching wine made you weak, which is why he is always pouring wine on you. He has told me all about that."

"I suppose that does explain his desire to baptize me with wine every time he sees me. He didn't do it today, though, because he didn't want to ruin the nice new clothes he gave me for this great celebration."

"Samson, I loved you, but I was afraid of him. He scared me so badly I did not know what to do."

"Not to mention the nice sacks of money you got."

"Yes, I know. I did want the money. It meant security for the rest of my life. That does not come easy for a woman."

"I could have given you all the security you ever needed. My father has more money than Phicol could even imagine."

"You never told me that! How was I to know? You didn't ask me to marry you either. What did I know about your family or what would happen to me if you were killed? I am sorry, Samson. I wish we had it all to do over again, but we don't."

"No, that is all over now."

"I had better go back. They will be missing me."

Samson hesitated and then he said, "Don't go, Delilah."

"What else is there for us to say?"

"Just that I do forgive you. I suppose it was just as much my fault as yours. You are right. I should have married you, but I was afraid also. Yes, I, the mighty Samson, was afraid. I had already been betrayed twice by women. I didn't know who I could trust so I trusted nobody. I am sorry. I should have married you and taken you back to my home. You were so beautiful! I wish I could see you one more time."

Delilah drew close to Samson now and reached out and touched his face. She, too, traced her fingers along the lines of his scars with tears streaming from her eyes. "You can still see me, Samson. In your mind's eye, I will always be there and will always be yours."

Samson took her hand and kissed her fingers.

"I have something else to tell you, Samson," Delilah said.

"What is it?"

Delilah pulled Samson's head down to her and whispered in his ear. As he listened, a smile appeared on his face. He kissed her again on her cheek. "Delilah, if you love me, you will do one last thing for me."

"What is it?"

"How did you come here?"

"In my own chariot. I drove down from Timnah, where I have been staying for a few weeks since I came back from Egypt."

"Where is your chariot?'

"Right behind the temple. There is a special place there where all of the chariots of the commanders are parked."

"Good. Then you have to leave this place now. Do not go back to Phicol."

Suddenly, Samson turned his face upward. In the distance he heard *Tap-tap-tap. Tap-tap-tap. Tap-tap-tap-tap-tap-tap-tap.* "Zetham?" he called in a low voice.

"I am here, my brother."

"That is Mother. It is time for you to go."

"Mother?" Delilah asked. "Whose mother?"

"Mine," Samson responded. "She and my father were here, but they are leaving now. That was their signal. You must leave also, Delilah."

"Why? What is going to happen?"

"I do not know, but if you ever loved me, you will leave now. Get away from here and away from the Philistines. Go back to Egypt or anywhere else, but get away from here. Promise me you will leave. Zetham is my brother and my priest. He will show you the way out."

"I will do as you ask, Samson, although I don't understand why."

"Thank you, my love. Now you have to go."

Delilah drew closer still to Samson. She placed her two palms against his chest and reached up and kissed his cheek. He ran his hand through her hair, pulling a few strands to his nose and breathing deeply.

"Go, my darling," he said. "Go now. Zetham, show her the way."

"Alright. But I will be back in a moment."

Zetham led Delilah away. In just a few minutes, he returned.

"She is gone, Samson."

"Now you, too, my brother."

"Will you not let me stay with you? Phicol promised to let me go!"

"Never mind what Phicol promised. He is a breaker of promises. You have to go, my brother."

"But what are you going to do? Why must I leave?"

"Listen to me, Zetham. On the day that the Angel of the Lord spoke to my parents, my mother said that she vowed I would be a Nazirite till the day of my death. That day has come, my brother. I came into this world alone, as we all do, and I must leave it alone. You cannot come with me now. Phicol will not set me free and probably not you either. I am sure that he plans a grand end to this feast by slicing my throat the way he did those children and then burning me on the altar. I hope I can give him a surprise first. You must understand that I will not be at peace unless I know you are away and watching over my parents. Please, my brother, before Phicol comes back. Please go."

"I will go, my brother," Zetham said. "I will not be happy, but I will go."

Zetham came around to the front of Samson and hugged him. Samson lifted him up off the ground and hugged him back.

Zetham gasped. "Be careful, brother, or you will squeeze the life out of me!"

Samson put him down.

"Zetham, I love you. I could not have asked God for a better brother. When I was a boy, I wished that I had a brother. Now, here when I needed him most, God sent him. Go in peace, my brother, and know that I go with you, as does our God."

"Good-bye, my brother." With tears in his eyes, Zetham turned and left.

Now Samson was truly alone and had never felt so alone in his life. His heart was aching, and he longed to cry again, but he knew the time for crying was past. He felt as though a great weight had been lifted from his shoulders, and now he was tired. He sank down to his knees and listened to the revelry above him. The musicians were playing wildly, and there was laughter and clapping and shouting. Samson turned his face toward heaven.

"My Father God," he said. "How I have failed You. Forgive me my sin, oh Lord. My sin of vanity and pride and a self-serving attitude. I am not worthy that You should do anything I ask, but oh my sovereign Lord, remember me, Samson, Your servant. Oh God, please strengthen me just once more, and let me with one blow get revenge on the Philistines for my two eyes."

Samson stood up. In the far distance he could hear the voice of Zetham. "Aww, aww, aww!"

"Aww, aww, aww!" Samson responded. "Ah brother Zetham, God bless you!"

Samson pulled off his cloak and tunic and stripped off the fancy boots. Now he was dressed as when he had first come to Gaza, in just his loincloth. Then Samson raised his head toward the floor above him and cried out in a loud voice, "Phicol, Phicol the coward! Phicol the yellow coward come down here to Samson! Phicol the dead man come down! Samson is waiting for you!" Samson listened. The music had stopped, and it was now quiet above him. He smiled.

At the sound of Samson's voice, the Philistines had looked toward the head table where Phicol and the governors were seated. Phicol stood and held up his arms.

"Do not be distressed, my friends. Our guest Samson has been known to need attention from my whip from time to time. I will handle him. Go on with the feast."

Samson's voice came from below them again. "Phicol the coward, are you coming? Phicol the faker, who hid behind the skirts of a woman. Phicol the pretender, who said he defeated Samson but needed a woman to do his work for him. Phicol the fool, who plays at being a general. Phicol the cuckold, who offers his wife to Samson for stud service. Bring her down, Phicol, bring her down now. Bring down your cow, Phicol. Samson the bull is ready! Come down, Phicol the lame and weak, who could not even whip poor Samson to death when he was shackled before him. Come down, Phicol!"

Phicol slowly descended the steps of the temple, rage burning within him. Samson had broken his word, and he would pay. Phicol, followed by many of his soldiers, stood before Samson, who could hear his labored breathing.

"Are you there, Phicol? Did you bring your wife? I am ready for her now."

"Ah Samson," Phicol said, struggling to control his voice. "I should have known better. You never change, do you?"

"I just wanted you to come down so I could share my last riddle with you."

"Whatever you have to say, it will certainly be your last words, Samson."

Then Phicol lashed out with his whip. As he had done before, he struck Samson again and again. It was a new whip this time, specially made for this ceremonial day, with a golden handle and silver strips on the edges of the leather. He hit Samson until his arms hung at his sides.

Then he gave the whip to one of the soldiers and pointed for him to continue. The soldier whipped across Samson's face until it was a pulpy mass of blood and flesh. He, too, grew weary and handed the whip to another soldier. One by one, they took turns until Samson's chest and face was cut into ribbons and pieces of bloody flesh hung from him. Still, he stood straight and tall. He smiled and did not flinch from the blows.

"Are you done, Phicol?" Samson asked.

"We are almost done," Phicol said. "Do you still have a riddle?"

Samson smiled. "Yes, Phicol," Samson mumbled through bloody lips. "One last riddle. You see, we are going on a great adventure today, you and I. I have always loved adventures. This will be my last, and you will go with me."

"You are going nowhere. You will not leave this temple alive. In a few minutes, we will drag you over to the altar and offer the great and mighty Samson up to Dagon. I planned to save you for the end of the feast, but now we will not wait. No doubt, you will bring us good crops for many years to come. You brought good fortune to me, Samson, and now you will bring it to all of the Philistines. I do not see your priest around, but when I am done with you, I will find him and kill him also since you have broken our bargain. Then, my friend, I will drive my way north into your country and find your dear mother and father. They, too, will be sacrificed to Dagon!"

Samson laughed. "No, Phicol. You see, this is my adventure, not yours. Have you guessed the riddle? This one is really quite easy. No secrets about lions and honey now to be stolen from me. Just a simple riddle. What is the great adventure we are going on, Phicol? The greatest adventure of all?"

"You are a fool, Samson. You are just babbling. Loosen the chains, and bring him to the altar now. I have had enough of this." Phicol turned and began walking to the other end of the temple. Samson could hear his steps retreating.

"No, Phicol, no! Wait! Here is the answer. I will tell you what the adventure is!"

Phicol turned back and stood still again in front of Samson. "Go ahead then, you idiot. Tell me your foolishness," he said.

Now Samson spoke slowly, carefully releasing each word, one by one. "The adventure is this, Phicol. Today, yes, this very day, you and I are going together to meet my God!" With that, Samson placed his hands on the two columns beside him and, with a mighty push, yelled, "Aww, aww, aww! The eagle of Dan and of the Lord God."

Phicol saw the columns move. Samson pushed again.

"Stop him, you fools!" Phicol yelled.

The soldiers rushed forward, pulling out their swords. Phicol grabbed a goblet of wine from the hands of one of the soldiers standing near him and splashed it in Samson's face. Samson laughed again, long and hard. Then he gave one final push, and the column on his right toppled over and then the one on the left. Phicol saw the floor above him coming down on his head. It was the last thing he saw on this earth, with a look of horror fixed on his face.

Samson, too, turned his head upward. He could not see the floor coming down, but he could hear it, and for the last time in his life, he smiled.

Down the road from the temple, Zetham was watching. He could see inside the temple and saw the two center columns move and then fall. Then the whole building shifted to one side and all the outer columns fell toward that side as the upper floors collapsed. Next to him stood Manoah and Zelponi. Zelponi gave out a loud scream, and Manoah hugged her to himself.

Zetham took a few steps toward the temple and fell on his knees, crying. "Oh Lord God, receive my brother Samson unto yourself," he sobbed. Then he leaned over and buried his head in his hands.

The dust from the temple's collapse rose and spread out toward them.

Zetham stood up and turned to face Manoah and Zelponi. "Come, Mother and Father. We must leave now."

"Yes, Zetham," replied Manoah. "We will leave now, but we will return. Samson's brethren will come back with us and get his body from beneath that temple."

Manoah and Zelponi climbed into the cart that Zetham had gotten from the corral. Zetham got up in the front and took the reins. "Come on, boy," he said, shaking the reigns. "Let's go home." Then Zetham began to sing. "I once walked bold like a man alone …"

When Manoah, Zelponi and Zetham reached their home, word was sent out all across the land of Israel. The message was simple. "We are going down to Gaza to bring home our brother the hero, Samson. Send soldiers to escort us."

From all over the land, each tribe gathered men to send. One thousand men from each of the tribes came to Zorah and camped in the grain fields, waiting for the word to march.

The men of Judah took the lead. Akim of Judah directed the tribes to order themselves in columns. As they had marched out of Egypt, they now marched on the road to Gaza. Each tribe displayed their banners, and the procession looked like a joyous parade, but it was a solemn one. The men were commanded to keep silent as they marched.

The Philistines watched the stream of men passing through their land in fear. Their leaders had all been killed, and the soldiers remaining in the land feared to act against this huge force of men.

When they came to Gaza, they divided themselves into work crews, laboring day and night with ropes and hoists to clear away the rubble and uncover their brother. Finally, they came to Samson's crushed body.

Phicol lay near him. Gently, they lifted Samson out and laid him on a long, white chariot. They washed his body, covered it with fragrant herbs, and wrapped him from the neck down in strips of linen. Then they began the march back home.

As they reached their land again, the people of Israel came out to see their hero. All along the road they stood as the lines of men passed. They carried banners and flags with the emblems of their tribes. As Samson's chariot passed, they cheered and waved the banners and then bowed their heads and said a prayer of thanks to God.

The day of Samson's burial was a day of great celebration. Manoah sent for supplies to feed the thousands of soldiers who were still with them. A great feast was held, and men ate in the fields that spread out from Manoah's house. There was dancing and singing. Most of the singing was about Samson, and how he had done in one simple act all that God had said he would do.

The night before his burial, Samson was laid on a table in his own room, and Manoah, Zelponi and Zetham stayed with him through the night. Zelponi washed his hair and rubbed oil through it. Then, sitting on a low stool at the end of the table, she braided his hair one last time, softly singing, "My little boy, my little boy, Samson is my little boy. Rest your head softly now, my little boy."

In the morning, the twelve tribes lined up in a long column, leading from the front of Manoah's house all the way to the tomb. Like a great pageant, pennons streamed in the blazing sun and banners fluttered above their heads. They were all silent, their heads bowed as the wrapped body of Samson passed in front of them. At the tomb of Manoah, Samson's body was gently lifted and placed on the marble platform in the center of the tomb.

The High Priest had wanted to give a speech, but Manoah had refused him. He said that Zetham would speak for his family and sing the song of Samson. All of the men gathered there had been given tiny fragments of parchment with the words for the song's chorus written on them. At Zetham's signal, when he was done speaking, they would all sing it together.

Zetham stood before the huge crowd gathered at the tomb and raised his hands toward the sky. Then he spoke.

"My Lord God, we bring to you today my brother Samson, one of your mighty men. He has fulfilled the task you set for him in this life and now he has returned to you. We will always be grateful to you that we had him for this brief time. Now Father God, into your hands we commend his body, soul and spirit."

Then Zetham sang the words to the song of Samson. When he had finished the last chorus, he waved his hand high over his head and all of the men joined him in singing the additional chorus that he had written.

"Oh Lord, dear Lord You're the mighty King.

Oh Lord, dear Lord, hear our plea.

We bring Samson, the Godly to you and sing

Pardon him oh dear Lord and pardon me.

Pardon him oh dear Lord and pardon me."

Then a huge stone was rolled in front of the opening to the tomb and sealed all around with clay and pitch. Zelponi approached the stone, and sobbing, placed her hand against it. Then Manoah and Zetham led her back to their house.

SAMSON: THE TOMB

Zelponi sat at the table in the back of her house, looking out the open rear door across the veranda to the fields and hills beyond. There was a high mound rising up before the hills with a huge round stone at its base. Behind it was the tomb of her husband, Manoah. A tomb he had built at a great price with the money he made selling weapons to the Philistines, who had been the cause of his son's death. Now, there lay Samson, waiting for her and Manoah to join him.

His cut, battered, and crushed body, washed and anointed with perfumes and oils and eyeless from its sojourn into Gaza, lay wrapped in funeral cloths. His muscles would never flex again. His laugh would never boom out over the hills of his youth again. His eyes, long since smashed and eaten by the ants, would never look again upon the face of his little mother who loved him so much. Zelponi groaned and rested her head on her arms. Every evening she sat like this as the sun set beyond the hills where Samson lay.

Now she heard a faint tapping on the front door of the house.

A long procession of people had come past their door since they returned from Gaza with Samson. When he had first been captured, their fellow Israelites scorned them. They were considered cursed, as their son had disgraced himself. The other judges in the land refused to visit them or even send their condolences. They said that Samson had failed in his task as a judge, and that with all his mighty power, he had squandered his gifts to please himself. This had hurt Manoah, who had always stood in high esteem among his fellow Hebrews.

But now, with the destruction of the temple in Gaza, they saw that what Samson had done in his death had indeed accomplished the task God had set for him. In one stroke, he had destroyed all of the Philistine army leaders, generals, and governors, demoralizing the Philistines.

Now the Israelites, for the first time in many years were talking about throwing off the yoke of the Philistines and even taking over their cities. But Manoah didn't care about their talk anymore. He had heard enough of it. Now, like Zelponi, he sat each evening in the quiet of his house and waited for death to reunite him with his son. Zetham, too, was there. His place in the evening was a low stool just outside the rear door, staring like Zelponi at the distant tomb of Samson.

Zelponi stood up and walked to the front door. When she opened it, she saw a woman holding a veil over her face standing in the doorway. She was dressed in silks from the East, finely brocaded and full of color. Beside her was a small child, a boy with long, black, curly braids of hair.

"Welcome, Sister," said Zelponi. "May I help you?"

"Are you the mother of Samson, the mighty man of Israel?" the woman asked from behind her veil.

"Yes, I am Samson's mother. Who are you?"

"It does not matter who I am. I have come a long way to see the parents of Samson, and I hope to learn about his God. For surely his God must be the one true God. What other God could destroy an entire temple with only the two hands of one man? I wish to know this God of Samson's and make him my God as well."

Zelponi stepped back into the house and motioned the woman to come in. She moved slowly through the doorway, still holding tightly the hand of the little boy by her side with one hand and the veil over her face with the other.

From the back of the room, Manoah stood up and emerged from the dark corner where he had been sitting. Looking over the head of his wife, he glanced down at the little boy. He tried to speak but could not, as the words stuck in his throat. Zetham approached from behind him and stared also, a hint of recognition in his eyes. He sniffed at the air.

"And this little boy?" asked Zelponi. "Is this your son?"

The woman nodded, and her eyes filled with tears. She lifted the boy, dropping her veil as she did so. From behind Manoah, Zetham gasped. The little boy looked across the room and saw the golden shield with the eagles and the serpent etched on its surface hanging on the wall. In it, he could see his reflection, held in his mother's arms. He laughed, a loud and infectious laugh.

"Yes," said Delilah. "This is my son, my little Samson."

EPILOGUE

Delilah's and little Samson's coming to live with Manoah, Zelponi and Zetham breathed new life into their household. No longer did Manoah and Zelponi sit waiting to die. They now loved their little grandson as they had loved their son.

Delilah, true to her word, became a student of the one true God. She visited with the priests often and studied the books of the law. The priests were amazed at her quick learning. They were even more amazed at the large sums of money she gave for the support of the priestly teaching. Together with Manoah and Zelponi, she paid for the construction of a home for widows and orphans. Here, the old and young alike could live in comfort, learning the precepts of God and His holy people. Delilah and Zelponi visited the home regularly, bringing food, clothes, and supplies for the comfort of the residents. They became known as angels of mercy to the poor and downtrodden.

In the course of time, Delilah was loved by all of the Hebrew people who knew her. Although they did not know the details of what had transpired between her and Samson, they knew that he had loved her, and so they loved her.

In front of Samson's resting place, Manoah planted a large field of wheat in long, straight rows. There, he, Zetham, and young Samson would often play among the ripening grain. One day, little Samson began running, his arms outstretched, crying, "I am Samson, King of the Eagles! Aww, aww, aww!"

Zetham followed him, yelling, "No, I am Zetham, King of the Eagles! Aww, aww, aww!"

And Manoah came behind, despite his age, still able to run, although at a slow, shuffling pace, yelling, "No, you are both wrong! I am Manoah, King of the Eagles! You are just little princes! Aww, aww, aww!"

The three of them ran among the golden sheaves, laughing in the shadow of the huge round stone with a single name carved across its top:

ƧAMƧON